Cooking Up Love

by

Candace Shaw

DEDICATION

To my husband. Success doesn't mean anything without you.

CONTENTS

ACKNOWLEDGMENTS

I would like to thank my dear husband for all of his love, encouragement and support during this process and adventure with me. I love you. I would also like to thank my family and friends for your continued encouragement. I sincerely appreciate it and I love you all. Thank you to my critique partners, authors Delaney Diamond and Sharon C. Cooper, for listening to my ramblings and helping me work out the kinks when my brain was too tired to think. Love you both.

CHAPTER ONE

"This is so delicious. Do you think they'll let me have another one?" Shelbi Arrington asked the waitress at Chow Bella's Italian Restaurant after she took the last bite of the tiramisu, savoring every sweet, sinful taste of the delectable dessert her hips needed to stay away from.

The waitress gave a sneaky look around the restaurant, then leaned over and whispered to Shelbi, "I'll see what I can do." She winked and hurried to the kitchen.

Satisfied with the response, Shelbi placed the to-go bag, which held the rest of her uneaten lunch, on the chair next to her purse. She had a habit of leaving her doggie bags and made an effort to remember this one. Her uneaten portion would serve as lunch tomorrow. She took out her iPhone and typed a few notes before tossing it back into her purse.

Shelbi rested her elbows on the checkered red-and-white tablecloth, making mental notes of the patrons and the decor. A few wrinkled their noses, one couple called a waiter over in disgust, and a group of businessmen checked their watches as they waited for the check. A party of eight in the corner booth was being serenaded with "Happy Birthday" by the waiters. Her favorite scene was of a small boy talking louder than anyone else, yet his parents still conversed and neglected to quiet him. The customers seated near gave the couple frosty stares, but they never noticed.

The waitress returned with a small bag, which she set on the table along with the check. She winked, and Shelbi winked back. She eased the smaller bag into the larger plastic one and tied the handles into a tight knot.

"Ms. Arrington, here's the check. Your lunch is on the house, but the manager thought you may want it in case you need the information for your article."

"Thank you very much, Lizzie." Shelbi took the slip of paper from the black leather receipt holder.

"You're quite welcome, Ms. Arrington. I feel honored to have served a famous food critic," Lizzie said before leaving to serve another customer.

Shelbi laughed. As a contributing food critic for *Food for Thought* with *The Memphis Tribune*, she was nowhere near famous. Some of her articles were featured in the newspaper and on their website. Plus, she had a large number of followers on her personal blog, *Food Passions*, which she started during her undergrad years at Spelman, but she wasn't famous.

She pulled her last five-dollar bill from her wallet, as well as all of the quarters at the bottom, and placed the money on the table.

Checking her watch, she had five minutes to dash to the next trolley that would take her home to her loft apartment at Central Station. There, she could kick off her heels, sip a latte, and eat the other tiramisu—sure to go straight to her hips—and type the article on the Italian restaurant and the other one from a few days ago.

Once at the trolley stop, Shelbi realized she had given all of her quarters to Lizzie. She dug around her purse for some loose change or a dollar, but all she found were eight pennies, her checkbook, and a half-eaten bag of Skittles. It was a fifteen-block walk from the trolley stop to her loft. She'd made the trip several times in tennis shoes with her jogging partner, but never in her sister's Christian Louboutins and a dress.

The red trolley stopped in front of her, and the door slid open. Unfortunately, it wasn't the trolley driver who had a crush on her and gave her free rides whether she had money or not. She hoped the driver would have pity on her.

"Good afternoon...um..."—she glanced at his nametag—"Mike. It seems I have given all of my change as a tip to the waitress a few minutes ago. All I have are these few..." She stopped to hold out her hand. "Pennies."

The driver tilted his head to the side and looked down at her hand. "All you gave the waitress was some change?" he asked in a harsh tone.

Stunned at his remark, as well as embarrassed at the line of people behind her groaning impatiently, Shelbi didn't know what to say or do. She checked her wallet, hoping she had a dollar hidden somewhere.

"Move it, lady!" a man behind her shouted.

"Hurry up!" a lady with a crying baby screamed.

"I have a slice of tiramisu you can have," Shelbi whispered. "Never mind." She turned to go before she said something rude, or worse, cried from embarrassment.

"I'll take care of it," a deep, concerned voice to her left said. A whiff of intoxicating cologne floated by as the considerate stranger dropped a one-dollar bill into the trolley's money slot.

"Thank you." Shelbi looked up to see a chiseled, handsome face and a sexy smile that caused her breathing to stop. When their eyes met, an immediate rush of sensual excitement washed over her skin. She glanced at his hand that had just placed the money in the slot. No wedding ring, but it didn't mean he was single. A man as chivalrous as him probably had women chasing him all over Memphis.

"No problem." He placed his hand at the small of her back. "Let's go sit down." The warmth in his voice and his kind gesture made Shelbi forget about her embarrassing moment.

3

While on their walk, Shelbi assessed his at least six-foot-one muscular frame, curly yet wild black hair, and a fair complexion with a slight tan as if he had just come from the beach. He wore jeans with a rust-colored corduroy jacket and a cream T-shirt, perfect for the first day of fall.

Shelbi was used to the take-charge kind of guy thanks to her dad and her two overprotective brothers. However, the way the stranger glanced down at her, giving her a comforting smile, made her heart skip a beat or two and was anything but brotherly.

Once settled in their seats, Shelbi turned toward him and once again was blown away by his strikingly handsome face. Her breathing unsteady, she tried to concentrate on the woman holding a baby the next seat over. Instead, her eyes were drawn to the good-looking stranger with dark, thick eyebrows and a neatly trimmed mustache with a slight beard growing in. He was sinfully delicious. If he were dessert, she would've devoured him right then and there.

"Thank you so much for paying my fare. Where are you getting off? I can pay you back."

He chuckled. "Baby, its only one dollar, but did I hear you say you have a slice of tiramisu?" He pointed toward the to-go bag in her lap.

"Why yes, I do, and you're more than welcome to have it."

"I'm teasing, but it's nice to know you were willing to give it to me."

Their eyes locked on his last four words. A heat wave rushed over her at the thought of *giving it to him*. Shocked at her thoughts about a stranger, she tried to stay focused.

"Well, you saved me from walking fifteen blocks in five-inch heels." Laughing, she stretched one leg for him to see the heels on her shoes—well, her sister's shoes.

"Hmmm…very nice…um, shoes," the gentleman said followed by a wink and a slight biting of his bottom lip.

Shelbi raised her eyebrow as she caught his curious eyes perusing her toned legs before they settled on her face.

"So what's your name?"

"Shelbi Arrington. And yours?

"Justin Richardson."

"Nice to meet you, Mr. Richardson."

She froze when their legs brushed as the trolley turned a corner, unleashing goose bumps all over her skin. She pretended to look out the window to hide the heat she felt rising in her face. She'd experienced these types of emotions before, but never within a five-minute time frame. In a few more moments, she would be at home, even though she really wanted to ride the trolley all afternoon with the handsome Mr. Richardson.

"I haven't seen you on the trolley before. Are you new to the area?" he asked, studying her face carefully.

"I just moved downtown about four months ago. Before then, I lived in Nashville."

"What brings you to Memphis?"

"I accepted a job at *The Memphis Tribune* as one of the food critics for *Food for Thought*."

His thick, dark eyebrows rose slightly. "You're a food critic? Critique any good restaurants lately?"

"As a matter of fact, I have. I went to Chow Bella's for lunch today, and a few days ago, Lillian's for dinner."

He nodded. "So, did you like Lillian's?"

"I can't answer your question. You'll have to buy a newspaper or go online to read my article on next Thursday," she said, smiling at him.

"Witty and beautiful. I like that. But I'm sure there's something you did or didn't like about Lillian's."

Shelbi hesitated for a moment. She really didn't want to tell a complete stranger, even though he did just rescue her from embarrassment and sore feet.

"Well, I was quite impressed with the atmosphere, and the food was delicious overall."

"Overall? What was wrong?"

5

"Nothing really. A few things could've been better. The barbecue sauce tasted a little bland, even though it's supposed to be the chef's special recipe. It seemed store-bought, and they don't serve pork, but this is Memphis, for crying out loud. Where's the pig?"

"Um…well, maybe the chef wants to try a healthier angle. Pork isn't good for your system. It isn't easy for the body to digest."

"I'll remember your tip the next time I cook bacon."

"So…" He stopped midsentence as Shelbi stood.

"This is my stop," she said disappointedly.

"Too bad. I really enjoyed talking to you."

"Me too. Thank you so much again for paying my fare." She stepped off the trolley and hesitantly glanced over her shoulder to see the fine-looking man one more time.

*****

Justin watched Shelbi saunter toward Central Station, a historic apartment building through which the Amtrak train ran. He strained his neck as far as possible as the trolley pulled away to steal a last glimpse of her lethal honey-coated body. Her red wrap-around dress revealed curvy hips, a plump bottom, and a small waist he wanted to wrap his hands around. She seemed refined, yet down-to-earth, with a naturally sexy air. He wanted to know more about the food critic whose sweet perfume still lingered in the atmosphere, making him high. A grin crossed his face as he remembered her flirty smile and the way she moved her shoulder-length brown hair behind her ear, making her little button nose even more adorable. He couldn't think of a time during his thirty-two years when he had met a woman like her before.

When he'd noticed her flushed, embarrassed face on the trolley, his protective side emerged. With music playing through his iPod, he hadn't realized there was a commotion until he looked up to see the cute side profile of a frustrated woman. He'd taken out his earbuds and heard her pleading with the driver about a tiramisu. The mean rants from the passengers outside of the trolley angered him and prompted him to help her. Unfortunately, he didn't get a chance to ask for her number.

While sitting with Shelbi, he'd missed his stop off of Beale Street, but it didn't matter. He was the boss, who was *supposed* to be on vacation, but surprising his employees and making sure the restaurant ran smoothly was on his agenda. He'd visited some friends in Pensacola Beach, Florida, for a few days, but now it was time to get back to work.

Moments later, Justin strode casually into his restaurant's front door, which should've been locked. It was four o'clock, so the restaurant was closed, preparing for the Friday dinner crowd at five o'clock. Normally, the servers would be setting their tables for the evening, but they were already immaculately set, which meant the waiters were in the locker room, chatting and playing around, but he didn't mind. They were hard workers who had helped his restaurant become a fine establishment.

Gold brocade toppers adorned black tablecloths under glass overlays and silverware rolled in gold napkins. Wineglasses and a candle in the middle elegantly finished the inviting table scene. The hardwood floors, original to the old building he renovated, shone brilliantly, and he smiled at the beauty of the main dining area. The brick walls rose two stories, ornamented with abstract pieces from local artists. The upstairs dining area was usually reserved for private parties or overflow on Friday and Saturday nights. The chandeliers shined brightly on him like a spotlight.

Even though Lillian's Dinner and Blues Club was a year old, he still had to pinch himself as a reminder—his dream was now a reality. A master chef, he had worked in gourmet restaurants around the United States and other countries over the past ten years, investing most of his money to open his restaurant in his hometown of Memphis.

Using his and his late mother's recipes, he turned Lillian's into a premier spot on Beale Street. He prepared Memphis Southern soul food, barbecue, and healthy gourmet dishes.

He sighed and gazed around his restaurant again as he remembered his mother's beautiful, warm smile and caring nature. She would've loved the decor and been pleased at the way he kept everything elegant and neat.

"I know you're smiling down on me, Mama."

"Um…excuse me, sir," a familiar male voice with a hint of sarcasm said behind him.

Justin turned to face his general manager and best friend, Rasheed Vincent.

"Back so soon, Jay?" Rasheed walked to the immense bar stocked with just about any liquor a patron would request. He sat on one of the barstools, and Justin joined him one barstool down.

"Looking good in here, Rasheed." Justin nodded his head and gazed around the restaurant. "I was expecting chaos."

"Man, you know I run a tight ship around here."

Justin chuckled and looked around once more. "Well, the fire department didn't call me, so I guess everything is fine."

"You know it is, man. Stop sweating. Have I ever disappointed you?" Rasheed's cell phone buzzed. He looked at the display and laid the unanswered cell phone on the bar.

"Well, I could think of a few…"

"Naw. Don't answer that question."

Justin nodded approvingly at his friend. "So, I'm impressed the dining room is ready. Where's Brooklyn?"

"Oh, she'll be out in a sec. Had to take care of some business or something."

"Really? And why is the main door unlocked? It shouldn't be unlocked until ten minutes till opening."

"Damn, man. I didn't realize…" Rasheed looked guilty as he walked toward the double glass doors.

"I already locked it, but please make sure it's locked in the future. If Brooklyn were here, it wouldn't be a big problem, but she's not. She knows it's Friday. Where is she, Rasheed?"

"Man, I don't know exactly. Somewhere in the back."

Justin didn't want to become frustrated with his best friend, but when he hired Rasheed's sister for the head hostess position a few months ago, he expected nothing but professionalism. He walked behind the bar and pulled a bottle of water from the mini-fridge below.

"Going to my office." Justin untwisted the cap and gulped a deep swig of the chilled water.

"Are you hanging tonight?"

"Yep. I may stick around for a while and do some work on my barbecue sauces for the competition." Justin couldn't believe the food critic told him his sauce was bland and tasted store-bought. It was his mother's recipe. He'd changed it slightly over the years and was working on a few others as well.

"Man, I'm excited about the Pride of Tennessee Barbecue Sauce Competition! This could really put us on the map! I can't believe they are upping the ante this year!"

"That's why I have to win." Justin leaned on the bar. "Just think, the grand prize will be a southeastern distribution contract, not just the state of Tennessee like last year. Glad I waited to enter this year's competition."

"Jay, you're going to win. I mean, who wouldn't like your sauce?"

Justin laughed sarcastically in his head. *Well, apparently a sexy little food critic didn't care for it. But what does she know?*

"Say, were you here when a food critic from *The Memphis Tribune* stopped by a few nights ago for a surprise visit?"

A wide, devilish smile formed across his friend's lips, which meant he was definitely present and had probably flirted with Shelbi.

"Yeah, man. Sexy little caramel-coated babe with hips…" Rasheed stopped to demonstrate with his hands exactly how wide Shelbi's hips were.

A sudden tinge of jealously crept into Justin's being at his friend's description of Shelbi. He was surprised, considering he'd only just met her, but for some reason he didn't want anyone else to think about her the way he did. Sassy. Witty. Cute. He wanted her all to himself, which surprised him even further. Though he had neglected to ask for her number, he was sure he could call the *Tribune* and ask for her.

"What did she order, and did she enjoy it?" Of all the times for him to be on vacation, a food critic made a surprise visit, and a sexy one at that.

"How did you know a food—"

"Don't worry about that. Did you greet her? Offer her an appetizer or two, drinks from the bar, dessert? What entrée did she have, and who prepared it?"

"Slow down with the twenty-one questions, man. The copy of the receipt is on your desk. Anthony prepared her dinner."

"Did she say anything?"

"Naw, man. She just typed some notes into her cell phone and took most of her food to go. I was the perfect gentleman in your absence."

"You asked for her number, didn't you?" Justin dreaded the answer.

Rasheed Vincent was a ladies' man. Female customers always scoped out the bald mocha Adonis, hoping he would give them the time of day. An ex–professional basketball player, he had more women calling and texting him than Wilt Chamberlain claimed to have slept with. If Rasheed were a rock star, women would literally throw their panties at him, and he would happily catch each pair.

"Nope. Not my type."

Good. Justin breathed a sigh of relief. He would hate to challenge his boy to a duel.

Justin was anxious to get back to his office to see the receipt, not because of the amount, but to know which of his recipes had touched her lips. He was disappointed he hadn't been in town to make the meal himself. He would love to cook for her, watching her pouty, kissable lips taste a dish he prepared. Maybe she wouldn't be so critical about his barbecue sauce and he could go into greater detail as to why he didn't serve pork.

"Was she alone?" he asked with a tight feeling in his chest. A woman as fine and intelligent as her probably had a man. *Lucky fellow to have all those damn hips to hold on to.*

"A distinguished-looking dude was with her, but I don't think they were a couple. He was too busy checking out all of the honeys, stealing my action."

"What's up, fellas?" The men turned to see their other best friend and restaurant manager, Derek Martin, stroll in. He joined them at the bar. "Just came back from the cardiologist."

"Are you all right, man?" Rasheed inquired with a concerned face.

"I'm good. That's why I go often, to make sure my blood pressure and cholesterol levels stay low. You know heart disease runs in my family, and yours too, Justin. You may want to go for an exam soon."

"I'll pass." Justin turned to go. He had work to do.

Derek chuckled in a sarcastic way. "Exactly, you will *pass* if you don't know you have a problem until it's too late."

"Derek, let's not start this conversation again."

"Man, I know you despise doctors, but…"

"Look, your mother didn't die at the hands of a surgeon who didn't try hard enough to revive her. Doctors don't care whether or not a patient dies. So no thank you, but I'm glad to know you're doing well."

"No problem, Jay. I just want to make sure my boys are healthy. You know we've had each other's back forever. You guys are like my brothers."

Justin had promised his childhood friends when he was finally able to open his Lillian's, they would be a part of it. Rasheed, the general manager as well as a part owner, and Derek, the business and financial manager, were the only people he trusted to help run his restaurant.

Once in his office, Justin noticed a business card paper-clipped on top of a receipt lying on his desk. He picked it up and was elated to see whose name was on it. The card was light pink with bold burgundy writing and *Shelbi F. Arrington* typed in a cursive font, but most importantly, it had her cell phone number. He turned it over and read a note, not so neatly scribbled: *Have your executive chef call me soon for an interview.*

CHAPTER TWO

Shelbi settled on her couch with her laptop, tiramisu, and notes about her dining experience at Chow Bella. She was going to change clothes and take a shower, but the masculine scent of Justin's cologne was on her, so she postponed her shower until later. It wasn't every day she had a man's scent on her, and figured she might as well enjoy it, especially a man as handsome as Justin.

She glanced at her watch. Her sister Bria, who lived a few doors down, was on her way over to hang out.

She read over her review of the Italian restaurant one more time. She wasn't as thrilled with their cuisine or atmosphere as she was with those of Lillian's, which would be the featured article for Thursday's list of places to dine and listen to blues. She really enjoyed the restaurant, minus the barbecue sauce. It was a little too bland for her taste, and it needed to be kicked up a notch. She scribbled the thought down for the article as a reminder to add it.

The ringing of her cell phone interrupted her thoughts. She glanced at the name Lillian's on the screen.

"Hello, this is Shelbi."

"Hi. This is Brooklyn from Lillian's."

Shelbi smiled as she remembered the nice hostess from the other night. "Hey, Brooklyn. How are you?"

Shelbi hit send on the e-mail to her editor for the article on Chow Bella. She grabbed her day planner from the coffee table and retreated upstairs to the bedroom, which could barely hold her full-sized bed and a dresser. The bedroom with the attached bathroom overlooked the living area of her sparsely furnished loft apartment.

"I'm doing well. My boss, Jay, is back from vacation and would like to set up the interview you requested."

"Great! When is he available?"

"He's very flexible and is willing to work around your schedule."

"How about tomorrow?" she suggested. That way, she could finish her article on Lillian's by the Monday deadline.

"That would be good for him. Say around noon? We aren't open until dinnertime, but he's always here on Saturday mornings creating new dishes."

"Perfect." Shelbi wrote the information in her planner and tossed it on the bed.

"I'll let him know, Ms. Arrington."

"Thank you, and please call me Shelbi. Saying 'Ms. Arrington' makes me feel so old. I'm only twenty-six."

"No problem. Jay is going to prepare dishes for you to sample, so don't eat anything, girl. The man can cook!"

"Tell him thank you for the opportunity and I'll see him at noon."

*****

"So what's for dinner?" Bria asked as she rummaged through Shelbi's refrigerator, pulling out the doggie bag from Chow Bella.

"I thought you were ordering a pizza." Shelbi poured two glasses of wine and then retreated with hers to the couch.

"Isn't it your turn?" Bria asked, opening the to-go container. She placed the chicken parmesan on a plate and then into the microwave.

Shelbi cut her eyes at her sister. "Are you being sarcastic? I told you I'm broke until payday."

"If you just start your residency…"

"Are we really going to have this conversation again? I swear you've mentioned it every day for the past five months."

"Shelbi, you graduated from medical school, yet you're a food critic. Are you forgetting that our family owns a medical practice? Your parents and your siblings work there. Does any of this ring a bell?"

"One more comment and you're leaving without the chicken parmesan."

"We're all worried about you. You excelled through Meharry, had outstanding reviews during your internship, and were accepted into a residency program that started two months ago without you."

Shelbi sighed and sipped her wine. She was expected to join the practice just as her siblings had. Their father, a cardiologist and surgeon, along with their mother, a general family doctor, opened Arrington Family Specialists when Shelbi was a freshman in high school. The twins, Cannon and Raven, were fresh out of completing their residencies when they began working for the family practice a few years after it opened. Cannon, a pediatrician, and Raven, an obstetrician/gynecologist, were exactly what the practice needed to become even more successful. Sean, a psychiatrist, joined two years later, and Bria, an allergist who focused on holistic health as well, just last year. The family expected it would be only a matter of time before Shelbi would join the practice as an endocrinologist. All she had to do was complete her residency.

"Why are you being so rebellious?" Bria asked, sitting on the couch next to Shelbi.

"I'm not being rebellious. What makes you say that?"

"You earned a culinary degree behind everyone's back while still attending Spelman and then accepted a food critic job after you graduated from medical school. You just threw away eight years of college to become a food critic. What's going on, Shelbi?"

"Nothing is going on. I'm a foodie. You know that. I love going to different restaurants, trying out new dishes for free. What could be better than that?"

Shelbi hated lying to her family about why she opted to become a food critic as opposed to continuing her medical career.

She hated reliving the real-life nightmare when a patient had been misdiagnosed by the attending physician. She had tried to explain to him he was incorrect because she had just written a paper on the illness, but he ignored her. Instead of going with her gut feeling and reporting it to the chief of medicine, she kept her mouth shut because she was only an intern and figured she was probably wrong anyway. The patient died a few weeks later from the illness she felt he had.

When the lifestyle editor from *The Memphis Tribune* came across her blog, Shelbi was offered a position as a contributing food critic for the newspaper. To ease the guilt and sort her thoughts out, she accepted the position instead of continuing her medical career after graduation.

Her parents were angry, but her siblings supported her new career endeavor, even though they still questioned her decision from time to time, as Bria was doing now.

"Can we change the subject?"

"Sure. Whose cologne are you wearing?"

Shelbi smiled as she thought about Justin again, but then frowned as she realized he hadn't asked for her number. She decided to tell Bria about her brief encounter on the trolley with the handsome man with the wild, sexy curls she wanted to run her fingers through.

*****

Shelbi knocked on the door of Lillian's a few minutes before her appointment. She ran her fingers through her hair and adjusted her laptop bag on her shoulder as she waited. Beale Street was definitely awake on a Saturday with tourists and locals eating lunch and listening to the blues at outdoor cafés.

One of the double doors opened to reveal a tall, dark man, with shoulder-length dreadlocks, wearing a blue polo shirt and khaki dress slacks.

"Good afternoon. Are you Jay?" *Two handsome men within two days.* However, this one hadn't kept her up the previous night wondering why she didn't give him her number. Nor did she witness the same electrifying jolt that ran through her body upon meeting Justin.

The man smiled and stepped back to let her into the restaurant. "No. I'm Derek Martin. One of Jay's managers." He turned briefly to lock the door. "He's in the kitchen preparing some samples for you to try, Ms. Arrington. Follow me."

"Thank you." As she followed Derek, she took note of places she wanted Jay to pose for pictures to go along with the article. Though she'd been able to get a few pictures at dinner the other night, she wanted a picture of the executive chef and owner as well.

"The kitchen is through that door," Derek said as he nodded toward the door and then turned back to the dining room.

Shelbi entered the kitchen and was engulfed by the delectable aromas. B. B. King and Lucille roared through the speakers of the small radio on a shelf above the stove. She recognized the song, "Caught a Touch of Your Love," from her dad's B. B. King record collection. The chef, whose back was to her, sung off-key, but it still made her smile. She didn't want to disturb him, especially when he turned the music up and sang into the spoon. She placed a hand over her mouth to muffle a giggle.

His crisp jeans showcased his thighs and butt, revealing the fact he was quite muscular and probably athletic. His broad shoulders filled out the white chef jacket he wore. The chef's hat was tilted to the side and waved back and forth as he danced. He gyrated his hips to the song as he stirred something in the pot. As much as she enjoyed his performance, she interrupted him.

She cleared her throat and tried to hide another giggle.

"Excuse me, but are you Jay?"

The chef turned off the king of blues, took off his hat, and twisted his muscular physique toward her.

"Why yes I am, Ms. Arrington."

Shelbi's heart raced as her breath caught in her throat. Falling back on the door to steady herself, her stomach tightened, and a heat wave charged through her. The man she tossed and turned over last night stood in front of her looking even more delicious than yesterday.

"It's you! The man from the trolley." She ran her fingers through her hair and hoped she didn't look like she felt— completely flustered.

"Yep. One and the same," he said, flashing a million-dollar smile. "Come sample this caramel sauce and tell me if it needs something else." He held out the spoon for her. "I'm experimenting with you today." His lowered voice held a hint of seduction.

I wouldn't mind him experimenting with me, but not in the kitchen. Well, maybe we could start in the kitchen and end up somewhere else...

A sensuous shiver raced through her. She tried to remain composed, but how could she when this fine, masculine man stood before her with a sexy smile, succulent lips, firm chest, and wild, crazy hair she just wanted to grab a hold of while he drove her up a wall. *Literally.*

She placed her belongings on one of the stainless steel prep counters and walked toward him, trying to shake herself from her fantasy, but her imagination was running rampant. She blew on the hot caramel before placing her lips on the spoon. He slowly inched the tip of it into her mouth as his eyes held hers in an intense stare. She closed her eyes and moaned as the sweet caramel with a hint of cinnamon traveled down her throat. She licked her tongue over her lips.

"Justin, this is superb. What dessert are you making this for?"

"Haven't decided yet, but it reminds me of you. Sweet, hot caramel with a touch of cinnamon, like your eyes."

Blood rushed to her face, and she hid her expression by leaning over the stove to open the stockpot on the back burner. A New Orleans low-boil consisting of crabs, shrimp, hard-boiled eggs, potatoes, onions, and corn on the cob smelled heavenly.

"This looks and smells divine."

"So do you," he answered in a seductive tone before turning off all the burners on the stove and stepping toward her. He was close enough to kiss her, and she almost wished he would. After last night's tossing and turning, she needed him to just hurry up and satisfy her longing. She stepped closer, and the enticing scent of his cologne, mixed in with his manly scent, filled her senses. She inhaled to take it in even more.

"Is the low-boil for me?"

"Yep. Hopefully, it will make up for my store-bought barbecue sauce you didn't like," he responded sarcastically.

A heat wave of fury washed over her skin, and Shelbi became annoyed at the handsome chef.

"I hope you aren't flirting with me just to receive an excellent review, because we can end this meeting now!" she snapped. She turned to gather her belongings.

"Look, lady, I don't need some young *contributing* food critic telling me my homemade barbecue sauce taste like it came from the grocery store. If you thought that, then maybe I should bottle it!"

His comment forced more anger from her, and she turned toward him as she waved her finger in the air and her down-home Memphis attitude came out.

"Well, then maybe you should bottle it along with your attitude." She stepped into his personal space, refusing to back down, the anger seething through her body. "First of all, I like your restaurant. Otherwise, I wouldn't have requested to meet the executive chef and owner. If I had known he would be an arrogant, pompous jerk like you, I wouldn't have wasted my time!"

Shelbi stared him down like a bull ready to send the matador flying across the ring with a swift blow to his butt. She hated being unprofessional; however, this man caused her to lose her cool. Heat rushed through her body, and apparently his as well, because she could feel the warmth radiating from him onto her skin. The room was silent except for their hearts beating fast and loud together in sync.

He stepped closer to her. Too close. The angriness on his face made Shelbi want to kiss him. Hard. Real hard. Little beads of perspiration had formed on his forehead, drawing his manly, intoxicating scent out even more. His muscular chest rose up and down, and his smoky eyes penetrated her, causing her breathing to stagger. His bold gaze held her entranced, and she couldn't unlock it, no matter how hard she tried.

Stay focused, girl. You're supposed to be mad at him.

He let out a long sigh and stared down at her, placing gentle hands on her shoulders. She thought he was going to kiss her and was prepared to respond willingly. Instead, he spoke in a calm and gentle tone.

"I sincerely apologize, Ms. Arrington. You're entitled to your *opinion*. Lillian's is my brainchild, my life. I've put my heart and soul into this restaurant. I'd understand if you don't want to continue with the interview."

"I accept your apology. I apologize as well. That was totally unprofessional of me." Shelbi stepped away from him and grabbed her belongings from the prep counter before she acted upon her thoughts.

"So, are you ready to interview me? I'll put on my chef's hat, not literally, and we can get started. Perhaps you can tell me your opinions of other dishes I have prepared especially for you today." He paused and made a call on his cell phone.

"Brooklyn, I'm taking Ms. Arrington to my office for the interview and lunch. Can you bring everything out in about ten minutes?"

He gave her a once-over while he was on the phone, lingering over her breasts, whose nipples had hardened. He ran his tongue over his lips, and his eyes settled seductively on her face. She was self-conscious of her jeans, simple yellow blouse, and sandals.

"I thought you put on your chef's hat," she said when he hung up with Brooklyn.

"I did, but I can't help it. You're wearing those jeans."

The heat rose in her cheeks again. "Thank you."

"My office is back here." They walked out a different door from the one she had come through to a hallway.

The masculine office consisted of an oak desk with two leather chairs in front of it, a leather couch on the right wall, and a dining table set for two on the left. Pictures of family and friends, cooking awards, and his degree from the Cordon Bleu hung on the back wall behind his desk. Shelbi pulled out her laptop and set it on his desk, next to a photo frame that contained three four-by-six pictures. The first was of a very beautiful woman holding a baby, the second one was of the same woman pushing a little boy on a swing, and the last picture, the same beautiful woman with a little girl.

"Justin, who is this lovely lady?" she asked as he settled into the chair behind his desk.

"That's Lillian, my mother," he said softly. "The last picture is my mother and my baby sister, Reagan."

"Your mother must be very proud of your success," she said, opening the file of questions on her laptop.

"I'm sure she's smiling down on me right now."

Taken aback, Shelbi looked up from the laptop screen and noted the wistful smile on his face. "I'm sorry. Forgive me." She rested her hand over his and caressed it softly. "You named the restaurant after her."

"Yes, I did. She taught me how to cook at a very young age. My mother cooked in many of the barbecue and soul food restaurants in Memphis. She always dreamed of us having a restaurant together one day, and had saved for it, but..." He looked away from her and inhaled.

"We can talk about something else."

"No, I want the history of the restaurant known. The menu options are a combination of her recipes and mine. I've changed some of my mother's ingredients to cook healthier and offer a variety. I don't cook pork, which I know is weird to you considering this city is known for pork and barbecue."

"I have to admit, I do find it odd, but you've just explained your reason why, and I can see how that would make sense."

Justin nodded and squeezed her hand gently before standing and moving to a bookshelf. He pulled out a black binder and handed it to her.

"This was my mother's original recipe book."

Shelbi opened the book to pages and pages of neatly written recipes. His mother's handwriting was just as beautiful as she was. Shelbi wished her handwriting was as neat, but it was always rather hurried and not legible. She handed the book back to him. He leaned on the desk in front of her, showcasing muscular thighs through his jeans. Shelbi held back a gulp and tried not to reach her hand over to massage the impressive muscles. She placed her attention back on her list of questions before she did something crazy like kiss him.

"So, what's your angle on cooking healthier foods, and how has your business prospered by offering healthy dishes?"

"My mother died of heart congestion when I was barely twelve and my sister was four. She had high blood pressure and high cholesterol." He stopped when a light knock sounded. "Come in."

Brooklyn opened the door and then rolled in a cart with covered dishes to the already set table. She nodded at Justin and smiled at Shelbi.

"Jay, everything you requested is here." She turned to Shelbi. "What would you like to drink? We have sodas, herbal tea, lemonades, organic fruit juices, or even something from the bar."

"I'll have iced tea." Shelbi was eager to get to the table. The aromas spewing from the dishes made her stomach grumble, reminding her she hadn't eaten anything since last night.

"Organic pineapple juice and two bottles of Fiji as well."

"No problem, Jay," Brooklyn said, closing the door behind her.

Justin held out his hand to Shelbi to escort her to the table. She placed her hand in his and stared up at his towering build. Everything, from his mesmerizing smile to the cleft in his chin, was adorable yet masculine at the same time. She was surprised at her minor flirting with him, but she couldn't help it. He was beyond fine, so she didn't mind him flirting either. He stepped into her personal space again, causing butterflies in her stomach to flutter around uncontrollably, destroying any hunger pains. When he raised her hand to his lips and kissed it softly, her heart thumped rapidly, as if she was listening to it through a stethoscope.

"You're a very beautiful woman, Shelbi Arrington."

*****

Justin stared down at the sexy woman in front of him. He hadn't meant to kiss her hand, but the effect she had on him was intense. He'd needed to feel her soft skin on his lips, and kissing her hand would have to do, for now. Justin lingered the caress of his lips on her as long as possible while staring into her cinnamon-brown doe eyes with long, silky lashes that grazed her flushed cheeks

"Th-Thank you," she stammered, withdrawing her hand away.

He pulled out her chair and let his eyes linger on her face once more. While he prepared their plates, Brooklyn quietly returned with the beverages. She promised to bring the desserts in thirty minutes.

He studied Shelbi as she took a bite of the shrimp and cheese grits. Her eyes rolled back into her head while she moaned, and he imagined her doing the same underneath him with her smooth legs wrapped around his waist.

"Justin, I've had shrimp and grits before, but never quite like this," she said, then took another bite. "I don't want the bowl to ever be empty. It's better than mine."

"I'm glad you're enjoying yourself." He pushed his plate aside and rested his hands in a crossed position on the table.

She sampled another dish as her eyes fluttered shut again. Her sweet, sensual moans turned him on in ways he couldn't even explain. If he weren't in a professional setting, he would've pushed the table out of the way and pulled her to him to settle her on his lap and devour her kissable lips.

Her sculpted face, a little beauty mark on her right cheek, and her pouty mouth partaking of the food he'd prepared especially for her, made him want to stare at her all day. She was sexy in skinny jeans that fit her curvy hips like a glove, and a yellow blouse enhanced her perky, rounded breasts, which rose and fell while she oohed and aahed over the meal. When she licked her finger after eating a shrimp, the bear in his boxer shorts rose and pointed directly at the sweet honey pot in front of him. Justin took a long gulp of his water to cool down the erection interrupting his business meeting.

Her sultry voice filled his ears like sexy jazz as she continued to compliment him on the meal.

"This is so good." She glanced at the plate he had pushed aside. "Why aren't you eating?" She took a swig of her water before continuing. "You didn't poison it, did you?" she asked with a laugh.

"No, baby. I sample as I cook. Besides, I enjoy watching you eat."

"Well, you definitely can cook. I see why your restaurant is so successful." She dabbed her mouth with her napkin and stood to retrieve her laptop from his desk. "I do have a few more questions."

Her hips rocked back and forth in the jeans, and he almost poured his ice water over his head to cool down the burning desire to kiss more than just her hand.

For the next hour, Justin answered all of her questions. Even though he tried to be professional, he was keenly aware of her graceful mannerisms, the proper way she held her fork, and her perfect enunciation of each word as she asked him questions. He was surprised at noticing things like that. Usually, he was concerned only about how fine a woman was, but with Shelbi, he was interested in the total package.

Her tongue ran over her lips as she savored the last drop of her meal. He imagined her tongue running over his lips, when a knock at the door interrupted his fantasy. Annoyed at the interruption, he dashed to the door wondering who in the hell had the audacity to disrupt him during his thoughts of kissing Shelbi.

He opened it slightly and peered out only to find Rasheed standing outside, texting as usual, with a wide Cheshire cat grin at whatever chick he was flirting with.

Rasheed looked up from his cell phone, smiling at his friend with a raised eyebrow.

"Why you so damn mad, man? You got a honey in there, don't you?" Rasheed cracked a smirk and stood on his toes, trying to peek into Justin's office, but Justin closed the door and stepped into the hallway.

Groaning in his head, he stared at his best friend, who apparently didn't get the memo not to disturb him during his meeting with Shelbi. "Is the kitchen on fire, Rasheed?" Justin crossed his arms in front of his chest and leaned back against the wall to hear what was so important.

"Naw, man. Carlos called," he said with a concerned expression. "He said he wouldn't be able to assist you at the cooking class on Monday. He had a family emergency and is flying out to New York tonight."

Justin volunteered at the community center in his childhood neighborhood every Monday afternoon. He taught high school students who aspired to be chefs how to cook delicious, healthy meals. He had the kitchen classroom built a few years ago for this purpose, and taught other cooking classes when time permitted. Justin was disappointed to hear his mentee wouldn't be available, but at the same time, he was concerned for the young man who had grown up in the Frayser area as well.

Justin sighed and nodded, contemplating another solution. Even though he could teach the class alone, he needed someone to assist with the nine high school students enrolled.

"Can you come? The class starts at three and will last a few hours."

"Man, you know I don't cook. You're the master chef, and I'm the master with the ladies!" He glanced down at his cell phone as it beeped. "Got one texting me now, and it's not even midnight," Rasheed said, walking away.

Once in his office, Justin sat down at the table with Shelbi as she typed away on her laptop.

"Everything okay? You don't look happy." Concern filled her voice, which made him feel better.

"Nothing major. I teach a cooking class at a community center, and my assistant won't be able to make it. I was trying to think of someone else I could ask at the last minute."

"You teach a cooking class? I'll have to add it to my article."

A lightbulb went off in his head.

"Shelbi, since you're a food critic who claims she can cook, how would you like to assist me? The class is this Monday at three."

"Claim? For your information, I could teach the class by myself. Sure. What are we making?"

"Roasted herb chicken with collard greens and a sweet potato pie, from scratch—not the can."

"I have a recipe for sweet potato pie that will have you begging me to cook dinner every night for you."

"How about I cook dinner and you cook breakfast?"

"I see the chef's hat is now off again."

"Well, the interview is done. How about we get together and cook, since you swear you know how."

"I can throw down in the kitchen," she said, leaning over the table closer to him and staring him in his eyes as if she was ready for a Western showdown. He leaned in closer as well, until their foreheads almost touched. "You name the time and place. I'll be there with my recipe book. If you want, I can show you how I make homemade barbecue sauce."

He let out a soft chuckle. "I'll be here tonight. How about tomorrow afternoon at my place?

"Your place?" she asked, raising an eyebrow.

"I promise to be a good boy."

CHAPTER THREE

Shelbi pondered Justin's "good boy" comment as she walked the few blocks from her loft to his condo in South Bluffs, which overlooked Tom Lee Park alongside the Mississippi River. She needed to walk off some calories after eating so much at his restaurant. Plus, he'd prepared a takeout bag, which she shared with Bria.

She wasn't exactly sure how she found herself in this situation. She hadn't planned to date anyone at the present moment, until she met Justin. He awakened a desire in her she had suppressed. She'd been hurt by a "good boy" who turned out to be a "bad boy," and she refused to go down that road again.

But her trust in men hadn't dwindled, for she knew there were some "good boys" still out there. Her big brother, Cannon, was an outstanding example, but her other brother, Sean, the proud president of Players United, had no intentions of settling down.

Shelbi admired Justin's ambition and determination, which reminded her of her own father, who grew up in the projects of downtown Memphis before the reconstruction of the area. Her father was a successful, renowned cardiologist and surgeon.

Like Justin, he gave back to his community through numerous organizations, such as the Distinguished Men of Memphis, in which he was the chairperson of the scholarship committee.

Once she arrived at Justin's, she took a deep breath before knocking on the door. Her palms had become sweaty on the handles of the grocery bag that contained the ingredients for the sweet potato pie.

The door opened, and Justin stood there, casually suave, wearing a long-sleeved black button-down shirt, a pair of jeans, and no socks. He had shaven his beard, but left the mustache and wild curls intact, just the way she liked them.

"Hey, Shelbi." He flashed a luscious smile as he held the door open for her to pass through. The foyer entrance had an antique table with a bouquet of white roses sitting next to a picture of his mother. A few abstract paintings adorned the walls, and through the foyer, an immense window framed the blue sky. The afternoon sun radiated throughout the room.

"You have a lovely home." She handed him her bag and rubbed her hands down the front of her dress.

"Thank you." He glanced around as if seeing it for the first time as well.

Shelbi followed him into the sunny living area with a few comfy leather love seats and a coffee table displaying a bunch of cooking magazines. She couldn't help but go straight to the window to see his view of the river. Breathtaking, the Mississippi River glistened like diamonds thrown throughout the water. She diverted her attention to the park, which was popular in Memphis for the festivals held every year, such as Memphis in May. It was her favorite festival, where barbecue restaurants from around the country competed to see who had the best barbecue. She had gone every year with her family for as long as she could remember.

"Your view is incredible. Do you sit here and admire it often?" She turned to face him and noticed the huge kitchen off the dining area. Justin had a chef's kitchen right in his own home: tall cherry wood cabinets, stainless steel appliances, including a chef's stove with six burners, and a water faucet on the wall for heavy pots. The huge island in the middle had a prep sink holding the uncut collard greens. The galley kitchen in her loft was cramped, with just enough space for one person to move around. She would love to have a kitchen of this grandeur one day.

"No, but I will now if you promise to stand in front of the window. But seriously, I do enjoy the view of the river. It's especially nice since I can see it while I'm in the kitchen—my favorite room, of course. Let me give you a tour of it since we'll be in here for the next few hours."

After Justin showed her where all of the pots, utensils, and spices were located, he opened a drawer from the island and pulled out an apron.

"You can wear this so you won't get your sexy sundress dirty," he suggested, holding out the white apron to cover her pink-and-green paisley maxi dress, which stopped right at the gold flat sandals she wore.

"Thank you."

"I have an herb garden on the patio. Would you grab a few sprigs of rosemary, thyme, and basil for the chicken? Also, I know we're making sweet potato pie, but I've been trying to perfect a chocolate swirl cake as well. Maybe you can offer your two cents since you think you can cook."

"I told you I can handle myself in the kitchen," she retorted in a playful manner. "I have a degree in culinary arts. Plus, I've been cooking since I was five."

"What did you make at five years old, little lady?"

"I baked cakes in my Easy-Bake Oven."

"Cute. I can see you in an apron, with pigtails and a little skirt, baking cakes. Of course, I'm imagining you at this age in that ensemble."

Embarrassed by his comment, she turned toward the patio to hide her wide smile and flushed face.

*****

Shelbi's hips swayed in a sensual rhythm under her sexy dress, which caused Justin to put on a thicker apron, hoping it would hide the monster of a rise in his briefs. The halter part of the dress left her smooth back exposed, showing a beauty mark below her right shoulder. The halter also revealed the outline of perfectly rounded breasts with the sides peeking out a little. He fought off the urge to pull her body hard against him and smother her lips and throat with hot kisses, then move to the split at the top part of the dress, where her breast rested.

He shook the images from his mind. Shelbi was there to cook, but it was hard to concentrate when he wanted to untie her dress and let it fall to the floor.

Justin pretended to dig around in the pantry closet, coaxing the bear in his pants to calm down. He had dated his share of women, but Shelbi Arrington was doing a number on him.

When he came out of the pantry armed with a few seasonings, he found her already rubbing the extra-virgin olive oil over the chicken. He strolled to the other side of the island to dice the onion and bell pepper to go along with the herbs inside of the chicken's cavity.

"Baby, when you're done rubbing that chicken down, you can rub my back down as well."

"You want me to stuff your mouth too?" She gave him a smirk.

"Well, that depends. What are you stuffing in my mouth?"

"I thought you promised to be a good boy."

"Oh, I'm very good. Never had a complaint, well, except about my barbecue sauce."

Shelbi shook her head with a grin and grabbed the vegetables and herbs to place into the chicken. She sprinkled the rosemary Justin had chopped over the chicken and placed the bird in the roasting pan. She washed her hands and placed the chicken into the oven.

"Would you like some wine?" he asked while washing his hands. "I have a mini wine fridge on the other side of the island. Grab whatever you like."

After Justin retrieved the glasses and opened a bottle of white zinfandel, the two of them began to work on the other dishes. She cut up the sweet potatoes to boil for her pie, and Justin washed and cut the greens. He decided this would be a great time to ask her about herself. She had learned mostly everything about him the day before during his interview, but he knew nothing about her except that she had lived in Nashville before moving to Memphis.

"So where are you from?" He placed some of the greens in the pot on the stove and turned back to look at her.

"Memphis, just like you. I grew up in Midtown."

"How long ago did you move away?"

"After I graduated from high school, I moved to Atlanta to attend Spelman. So about eight years."

"I didn't know Spelman offered a cooking degree."

"They don't. I earned an associate's degree in culinary arts at the Atlanta Institute while getting my bachelor's degree in biology."

"How did you manage that?"

"It was easy. I love cooking and eating. Going to the culinary school was fun for me, a stress reliever, even though it took forever to finish. Three years. I took one class per semester."

"I bet the student loan companies love you!"

She giggled. "Don't remind me."

"Why the change in careers?"

She stared off into space for a moment with a hesitant expression and then placed her cinnamon eyes on him, stirring emotions he hadn't felt before.

"I was the food critic for my college newspaper, and I also started my own food blog. So, are you going to cook some smoked ham or turkey with the collards?"

"Thanks for the reminder. And you know I don't use ham. The smoked turkey legs are in the fridge in a bowl. Could you get them for me and place them in the pot?"

"No problem."

He added the rest of the greens and placed the lid on the pot. She placed the cubes of sweet potatoes in a pot of boiling water. A whiff of her tantalizing perfume, mixed with her own scent, nearly knocked him over as she passed by him. *Time for another session in the pantry.*

"You know, Justin, I'm rather impressed how you run a fabulous and successful restaurant and still make time to teach a cooking class."

He smiled at her compliment and joined her at the island on the barstool across from her. "I grew up in a rough area of town. My mother worked two jobs to make sure my sister and I were taken care of. I managed to not get sucked into the gang life or selling drugs. A lot of my friends got caught up in that and are now either in prison or dead." He shook his head in dismay as he thought about the boys he grew up with. He was thankful Rasheed, Derek, and he had managed to escape that lifestyle.

Shelbi sighed. "I know what you mean. I have girlfriends from high school that got caught up dating drug dealers and thugs, and I have no clue where they are now."

Justin went to the stove and stirred the collard greens. "Your chicken smells good, girl! You put your foot in it!" He laughed out loud as she joined him at the stove, bending over to peek into the oven window. He almost sucked in his breath as she bent over in front of him. He walked back to the island before he did something foolish like place kisses down her tempting back.

"Mmm…it sure does. So do your collards. I've never used turkey before." She leaned against the counter next to the stove. "Finish telling me how you managed to escape the street life."

"When my mother had her second heart attack, she made me promise to not go down that path. She wanted me to get an education and still pursue the dream of our restaurant. She made me promise to never forget where I came from and to help those less fortunate."

Shelbi nodded her head in agreement. "Sounds like my father. He always says, no matter how bad you think you got it, there is always someone else with less."

"That's how my mother was. Growing up, we may not have had much, but my mother always shared what little we did have. If she cooked a big pot of gumbo, she shared it with the other people that lived in the little one-bedroom duplex we lived in for several years. If someone's water got turned off, she let people bring over jugs to fill up or take a quick shower if need be. She was kind and gracious." He stopped for a moment as his voice began to quiver. "I miss her very much."

"What about your father? You haven't mentioned him."

What father? He met his father only a few times as a child. When he was seven, his father had promised to be a dad to his son and ended up getting his mother pregnant again. When he found out, he skipped town.

Mr. Brown is what he called him whenever he spoke of him, because he couldn't even bring himself to think of the man as a father. The man didn't even have the decency to give his firstborn son his last name, child support, or a visit. He tried to contact his father a few days after his mother died, only to be told he had the wrong number. Justin hadn't looked back. It made him stronger, more determined, and he wanted to be a loving husband and father when the time presented itself.

"My father isn't in my life, but my grandfather and my uncles are my male role models.

But a lot of young boys don't have that. I teach the class at the community center to display a positive image to these young boys. I want them to see that even though they may be in that environment, it doesn't mean they have to stay in it."

"I think it's great what you're doing, and I'm glad I can assist you tomorrow."

"Thank you. My cooking class gives them something to look forward to after school instead of running the streets looking for trouble. Rasheed and Derek volunteer once a week as well. We grew up together."

"I'm glad the three of you are doing your part. Now let's finish cooking. I'm starving."

"Me too." *But not for the food.*

*****

"Are you ready for dessert?" he asked.

Justin took their empty dishes back to the kitchen while Shelbi lounged on one of the leather couches in the living room. Miles Davis soothed her with his sexy rendition of "In a Sentimental Mood." She took her shoes off and stretched her feet out on the couch while sipping on a glass of wine. She was quite proud of the simple yet delicious meal she and Justin had made, and she hoped the students tomorrow would enjoy preparing it as well.

Justin returned with the chocolate swirl cake sitting under his homemade vanilla ice cream, dripping with chocolate sauce.

"Now you know that's going straight to my hips," she teased, taking the plate from him. He sat down on the floor in front of her. "Where's your cake?"

"I'm full. Besides, I ate a slice of your pie with my dinner, remember?"

"No, you had two slices of pie."

"It was good, baby. You're right, you can cook. So why are you a food critic and not in a restaurant or a bakery?"

"I enjoy cooking, but I like eating and trying new things as well. If I worked in a restaurant, I wouldn't be able to experience a different culture or cuisine as I can when I go to a variety of places." She paused to take another bite of the cake. "This cake is delicious."

Chocolate sauce dropped from the spoon and rested between her breasts and Justin's eyes were instantly drawn there.

Her heart began to beat faster as his hot gaze lingered on her pointed nipples as they peeked through the halter.

"Umm…can you get me a napkin so I can wipe this off?"

"What? Oh, sorry. I was distracted." His voice had become heavy and serious.

"I asked for a napkin."

"I had hoped you would say my tongue, but if you really just want the napkin…"

Heat moistened between her legs, and she swallowed hard to catch her breath. Her breathing turned into little spurts at the thought of his tongue between her breasts, on her lips, neck, and any other place he wanted it to go as long as it was on her body, putting out the fire he provoked.

Justin took the plate from her trembling hands when she didn't answer. Joining her on the couch, he ran his hand up her arm to the back of her neck with a soft caress, causing her eyes to flutter shut at the gentleness of his touch. A light moan escaped her throat as his lips moved slowly over hers, savoring every bit of her with his tongue. Hot. Tender. Stimulating. Nearly gentle, except for the sensual flame of heat traveling through her body. Her nipples hardened even more, and her legs went weak. She clutched his shoulders for support, her head falling back as his tongue dance changed from tender and gentle to hard and feral.

Shelbi gasped. She'd never been kissed like this—so ravenously and powerfully, she couldn't keep up. She gave up trying and released herself to his commanding lips. Relief washed over her as she was finally able be engulfed by him, and she kissed him back hungrily to show she desired him as much as he desired her.

Justin moved to the chocolate splash between her cleavage and licked it seductively while his hands kneaded her breasts underneath the flimsy material. He pushed it aside, freeing the ample mounds, and sucked one of the brown nipples while cupping the other breast. The next thing she knew, she was on the floor under him. She wasn't sure how she got there, but didn't care. She placed her hands on either side of his head to bring his lips back to hers so she could taste his pulsating tongue once more.

Her fingers stroked his soft, wild curls, eliciting a hard groan from his throat. Liking his response, she swirled her tongue faster and more wickedly inside his mouth. She was quite surprised at herself for her behavior, but she didn't care. She'd wanted to kiss him the moment her eyes met his on the trolley, which was a first for her.

His kisses dropped back down to soft and tender again. His head raised, his lips lingered on hers, and she was disappointed that he stopped.

"I hope I wasn't too forward," he said. "You're just so damn delectable. I had to have a taste, and you taste better than any other dessert I've had."

"Yes, that was a mouthwatering dessert."

"Mmm…well, one day, I'll serve you the main course."

"How many courses are there?"

"Plenty."

"What time is it? You have to be at the restaurant for the late-night private dinner party."

"It's six. But, you forget, I'm the boss."

"Who likes everything to be perfect. I'll clean the kitchen while you get ready."

He kissed her gently one more time before helping her up.

Smiling, she turned up Miles and proceeded to clean the kitchen. She was in a pleasant, sentimental mood and couldn't wait to sample any other courses he served her.

CHAPTER FOUR

"Where were you? I've been calling and texting you for the past three hours!" Bria asked with more of a nosey tone than a concerned one.

Shelbi returned home to find Bria stretched out on her couch, laughing and eating the leftover Cajun low-boil. Watching reruns of the television show *Scrubs* in her pink scrubs, Bria seemed quite content invading Shelbi's space, as usual, without her permission. Shelbi's gaze fell on her sister's shoulder-length hair pulled back into a bouncy ponytail. Her clear bronze face shone brightly as if she had just washed off a face mask. *More than likely my apricot mask.*

"Comfortable?" Shelbi asked, sitting on the couch next to Bria, who eyeballed the bag in her hand.

Bria pointed to the bag, smacking her lips. "What's that?" Her dimples showed, and Bria looked as if she could be actress Gabrielle Union's twin sister.

"Chocolate marble cake." She handed her greedy sister the bag. Shelbi turned her focus on the actors who played Dr. Turk and Dr. Dorian on the flat-screen, hoping if she pretended to be half interested in the medical comedy, her sister would stop asking questions.

"You still didn't answer my question."

Shelbi sighed. *That idea apparently isn't going to work.* She knew her siblings meant well, but just because she was the baby of the family, didn't mean they still had to treat her as such.

"Minding my business." She kicked off her sandals and rested her feet underneath her.

"Shelbi, as your big sister, I just want to make sure you're safe. You always tell me where you're going, and you usually text me back within a few minutes. I just wondered where you were and why you're just getting home at eight in the evening."

"Big sister? Girl, we're barely two years apart. We've grown up together. We attended Spelman and medical school somewhat together, and now, you live three doors down."

"Speaking of…" Bria pushed mute on the remote and gave Shelbi a serious face.

"Sis, don't start again." Shelbi didn't feel like having this conversation. She'd just had the best kiss of her life, and Bria wanted to ruin it with talks of completing her residency. "In case you forgot, I did finish medical school and passed my licensure test. I have the title 'Doctor' in front of my name just like you."

"Oh really? Then why, when we went shopping last week, did I see you fill out the credit card application for Macy's and you just put down 'Miss Shelbi Arrington' and not 'Dr. Shelbi Arrington'? And why, when I look on your wall, do you have your degree from Spelman and your culinary arts degree proudly displayed with your other accomplishments, yet I don't see your freaking medical school degree! It should be under a spotlight and not in the back of your closet under boxes of my shoes that you keep borrowing. What gives, baby sis?"

Shelbi stared at the wall that held all of her accomplishments and awards since high school: first place in the swim meet, first place in the academic bowl, Who's Who

Among American High School Students, and numerous other plaques and certificates.

Shelbi was used to being successful. She never failed at any task she tackled. When the man died during her last semester of her internship, she felt as if she had failed him and herself for not making the attending physician listen to her.

Doctors in the hospital where she interned let death roll off their shoulders as if it didn't matter. They showed no remorse, and she didn't want to be a part of that environment or profession.

She was perfect at everything and anything she set her mind to, especially tasting and recognizing a well-cooked meal, but being a doctor apparently wasn't on the list. And she couldn't tell her family the real reason why she no longer wanted to continue in the medical profession. They wouldn't understand. They were all doctors.

"I like being in the culinary industry. You know I've enjoyed cooking since we were kids. I was always in the kitchen helping Mom or Mother Dear while you played doctor."

"I beg your pardon?" Bria raised her eyebrow at the last statement.

"You heard correctly. Playing doctor with your dolls, trying to operate on them, or dissecting worms and frogs. I wasn't referring to the times Raven and I found you behind the shed playing doctor with the little boy in your class."

"Ha ha. You're so funny, Dr. Arrington. I mean, forgive me, *Ms.* Arrington."

"Why are you here again when you have a larger, very spacious loft down the hall?"

"Unlike you, I can't cook, and I didn't want a sandwich, so I came to see what you had in the fridge. Glad I did. Where did the cake come from?"

"A friend," Shelbi answered, not wishing to discuss whatever she was doing with Justin. She honestly didn't know where their relationship was headed. She was going to go with the flow and learn more about him. Even though the thought of the next course made her blush all over again.

"Friend? Girl, we have the same friends, and they're in Atlanta. I know Jade and Tiffani aren't in town, so what *friend* is this?"

"One I'll tell you about later," she said smoothly, ready for her sister to go so she could take a bubble bath and think about Justin. "Now, take the cake and go home. I have an article due, and I would like to be done by tomorrow afternoon."

"That's right." Bria tapped her chin. "You're assisting with a cooking class with the fine healthy chef over at Lillian's. Is that the friend?"

"Yes, but it's not a big deal. We made dinner and hung out. That's all."

"Yeah right. I saw how you came in floating on cloud nine. Anyway, I need to go get ready for work in the morning. I have a patient coming in at seven before she goes to work." Bria stood with the bag of chocolate cake and her keys.

The same height at five feet five inches, but slightly smaller, Shelbi always wondered where on earth did all of the food go that Bria ate. She was a beanpole, but ate whatever she liked, and it never went to her hips. They couldn't share the same clothes since Shelbi didn't wear a size two, more like a size six. She had somehow convinced herself she was a four, but her daggone hips made her a six. Luckily, she could fit her sister's shoes just fine and wore them more than she wore her own.

"That early? The practice doesn't open until nine."

"I know, but if she's late, she'll get docked her pay. I don't mind. She's actually Raven's patient, but she's trying to have a baby, and Raven suggested I do acupuncture to relax her before Daddy comes. You know he prefers I don't practice holistic medicine."

"How long has she been trying?"

"A few months. She doesn't have any fertility problems, just stress, which I can help alleviate. Anyway, have fun with the chef. I ate at Lillian's when it first opened. He's hot!"

Shelbi smiled at the thought of his hotness all over her again.

*****

Justin checked over his grocery list before hopping out of his black Lincoln Navigator: four whole chickens, twelve bunches of collard greens, onions, and green peppers. He had a mini herb garden at the community center and already had the ingredients for the pie. He walked confidently, with a little extra pep in his step, into the Whole Foods with a smile on his face. He still beamed over the previous day with Shelbi and couldn't wait to see her at the cooking class. He was entranced by her lush lips, sexy moans, and ambrosia scent that lingered in his memory. She made him feel as if he should be jumping up and down on a couch professing his love for her on a talk show.

Justin had dated numerous women over the years. A few serious relationships here and there, but none of them kept trampling through his mind like the cute and sassy food critic. His thoughts traced back to yesterday, when she was on the floor under him. If he hadn't had to prepare food for a celebrity dinner party last night, he would've taken things further, but in a way, he was glad he didn't. She wasn't one-night stand material. He'd had plenty of those and even attempted to make a real relationship with them, but it never worked out. Something was always missing, and he ended up breaking things off early in the relationship.

His focus wasn't on women in his younger years, it was on establishing his career. After his mother's death, his main concern was being a good big brother to Reagan, owning a successful restaurant, and educating people on the importance of cooking and eating healthy meals.

Now he had met Shelbi, and something in him had changed. It wasn't just her pretty face, curvy body, and sexy attitude that drove him crazy. Her sassy and witty comebacks, her warm smile, and the bold way she stood up to him about his barbecue sauce turned him on even more.

His cell phone rang. Glancing down, Justin saw Reagan's name and picture flash on the screen. At twenty-four, Reagan was a wedding planner with an event firm in Atlanta. She reminded him of their mother with her sandy-brown hair, cocoa eyes, and bright, warm smile that matched her heart. He was very protective of his baby sister and disappointed when she chose to move to Atlanta after she graduated from the University of Tennessee.

"Hey, baby sis. What's up?" He grabbed a grocery cart and proceeded to the poultry aisle.

"Exhausted. I had a wedding this weekend, so I'm taking the day to relax. Plus, I'm not feeling well."

"What's wrong?" He stopped browsing the hormone-free chickens to give her his undivided attention.

"Stop worrying. I'm fine. I just have a nagging cold that won't go away. I'm going to the doctor tomorrow to see what's wrong. I may need a prescription. The over-the-counter stuff just isn't working."

"Reagan, I'm sure the cold won't go away because you're working so much and need to relax. Take some vitamin C. You don't need to waste your money going to a doctor."

Reagan sighed. "Justin, don't start again. All doctors aren't evil."

"I've never said they're evil. I just don't trust them because they don't care for their patients." He grabbed four whole chickens and placed them in the cart. A cute lady in front of him winked, but he wasn't interested. Sure, she was cute, but she didn't have Shelbi's cute dimple on her left cheek, or her pretty smile.

His sister sighed a groan and then paused. He knew his sister well—she was contemplating how to respond. She was the type who actually thought things through before saying or doing something, which he admired, except when it came to

43

him. He was ready to take the phone away from his ear to avoid the upcoming lecture he was bound to hear.

"Justin, when are you going to stop this fascination over despising doctors? I know—"

"You were too young to remember, but the surgeon could've done more to save Mama. She was so young, so beautiful, so perfect."

"I know, but things happen. I wish she was still here. I wish she could've seen me in my prom dress and at college graduation. I wish she was here to laugh and cry with me over heartaches, but I'm blessed to have you and our grandparents. Eventually, I'll get married and have children, and she won't be in the front row as you walk me down the aisle."

His sister always knew what to say to smooth things over, which probably helped with the pre-wedding jitters and cold feet of her bride and groom clients. While his view on doctors hadn't and wouldn't change, it dawned on him that his sister was a grown woman with a successful career, living a fabulous life in Atlanta. She was doing quite well, and he was proud of her.

"You make a good point, but that married and children thing is years from now, right? Is there some knuckleheaded boy I need to jack up in a corner?" he asked seriously. One scumbag had already broken her heart in college, and Justin wasn't in the mood to curse anyone out again, but he would if he had to. He loved his sister and wasn't going to let some asshole treat her wrong.

"Nope. And I gotta go. Having lunch with my girls and then shopping at Lenox Mall."

"I thought you were relaxing today."

"Shopping is relaxing. But I promise to take some vitamin C before I leave. Looking in Alex's medicine cabinet now."

"Alex? Reagan, I know damn well you ain't shacking with some man. Put his behind on the phone," Justin shouted at the top of his lungs. People in the produce section stopped what they were doing and stared at him. He grabbed a bag of onions and threw them in the cart and moved toward the checkout area as he thought about crushing Alex's skull in.

"Calm down! 'Alex' is short for 'Alexandria,' my roommate and soror. You met her, remember?"

"Oh yeah," he said, remembering her flirty roommate. She was fine, but not his type. Besides, he refused to date any of his sister's friends. "Well, be careful. Wear something on your arms. It's cooler now, and you don't want the cold to get worse."

"Okay, big brother. I love you."

"I love you, too."

After he placed the groceries in the trunk, he sat in his Navigator brooding over his conversation with Reagan. His sister had provoked thoughts about his distrust for doctors, but it wasn't all doctors, just the one who let his beautiful mother die during the middle of open-heart surgery. The doctor had promised before the surgery he would do his best to take care of their mother. As a child, he had believed the man he'd known since he was five years old. The doctor had donated uniforms to the Little League baseball team Justin played on and had attended the career day at his school. After the doctor told his grandparents of his mother's death, Justin had begged him to save her, wrapping his arms around the man's midsection, crying and pleading. Instead, the doctor had released him to his grandmother and walked away. Moments later, while he was still in the waiting room with his grandparents and other family members, Justin had spotted the doctor smiling, walking toward the elevator, wearing a black tuxedo as if all was good in his world.

Since that time, Justin felt doctors showed no remorse over losing patients. He had managed to avoid going to a doctor, minus the occasional physical only if necessary. A chime from his cell phone detoured his thoughts. A text message from Shelbi was on the screen.

See you soon. I'm leaving now to head to the community center.

He texted back: *Can't wait to see you.*

A wide smile formed across his face as he pulled out of the parking space and headed out to the Frayser area of Memphis. Shelbi was the kind of woman a man would want by his side in a committed, monogamous relationship. Only an idiot would let a woman like her get away.

CHAPTER FIVE

"Boys and girls, you did a great job today following the recipes and creating your delicious meals. As a food critic, I'm quite impressed. I would like to do an article on my blog and take some pictures of you with your entrées next week or the one after, once I have a parent or guardian signature on the picture release form."

The high school seniors had been enrolled in the class since June and learned a lot from Justin in just four months. Shelbi felt there were quite a few future chefs in the class. Of course, they were still teenagers who tried to sneak a text message here and there or flirt with each other.

After the two-hour cooking session, they spent an hour talking and eating the healthy dinner they made. The students asked Justin and Shelbi questions and received feedback on ways to improve.

Once the students cleaned up and left, Shelbi wiped down the tables and counters. She sensed Justin's eyes on her. Turning around to confirm, she noticed him leaning casually on the refrigerator with his white chef's coat draped across his shoulders while both hands rested in the pockets of his khakis. His stare was hungry, like a tiger ready to pounce and eat his prey. She took off the white chef jacket he'd brought for and laid it next to her purse on the prep counter.

Shelbi thought about her other white coat folded in a box in her closet. Her father had presented it to her at her graduation from medical school. Bria's prying had set her mind in a frenzy. But now wasn't the time to become emotional about her problem, when she had a fine man across the room staring her down as if she were naked.

Justin's red polo shirt showcased his muscles, which made her breasts ache, wanting to be free and meshed up against his chest—preferably his bare chest. He tossed his white coat on the counter and ran a seducing tongue over his lips as his eyes roamed over her jeans and beige T-shirt. Her bare arms tingled with goose bumps, and her breasts wanted to burst free of the flimsy T-shirt when Justin settled his eyes there.

"Are you leaving now?" she asked.

However, leaving was the last thought on her mind. She'd been completely professional during the cooking class, but now she wanted to be totally unprofessional.

"In a few." His voice was husky and laced with seduction. "You're gorgeous."

Shelbi sucked in her breath as his eyes glazed with passion for her, which caused her to go dizzy. She couldn't remember a time when a man had stared at her in such a manner.

She closed the gap between them and stood in front of him, rising up on her ankle boots to meet his lips with a deep, long kiss. She could taste the spices of rosemary and basil, intertwined with his masculine scent intoxicating her air. He grabbed her hard against him, wrapped one hand around her waist, and sunk the other one in her hair. Their tongues tangled together passionately as if it would be their last kiss. She pressed her throbbing breasts against his firm chest when the erectness of his growing arousal pushed through his pants. A deep moan escaped her at the thought of having his rock-hard shaft penetrate her tenderly and roughly all at the same time. She had been with only one other man, once in her entire life, and hated the experience, which lasted a mere minute. But she was ready to give it to Justin right now if he asked.

He gave her a sly smile and turned them so she was against the refrigerator. Justin placed kisses down her neck as he stroked her pulsing breasts.

"Justin, I really hate to stop what we're doing, but..." Her voice trailed off as he raised his lips to capture hers once more, this time even more intensely, to smother whatever she was about to say.

"Be quiet, baby." He claimed her lips once more, sending her into a whirlwind of passion. His kisses were more addictive than chocolate, and she matched them with the same intensity.

Justin wrapped his arms around her waist, matching her heated kisses with his own. He pulled her tongue further into his mouth, setting off a series of breathless moans from her. She removed her lips and placed sensual kisses on his neck, which held the intoxicating cologne he always wore, engulfing her further into his realm. She had been taken out of her world and was in his, with his controlling hands roaming over her body.

Shelbi had never been kissed before by a strong, virile man like Justin. He was passionate, tender, and commanding. She was sexually charged and had the urge to unbuckle his belt and send it flying across the room to get to the hard instrument she wanted to play over and over, until she was out of breath.

"Damn, Justin." Her breath was heavy as she sucked and licked on his neck to emphasize her words. She moved her hand down to his erection, which hardened even more as she massaged it through his pants.

But when Justin stopped the moment of passion, she was too dazed to hear what he said.

"What, Justin?" If he had said the kitchen was on fire, she wouldn't have been surprised because his kisses had ignited a fire all over her that could've very well exploded and set the place ablaze.

Knock, knock.

Shelbi jumped, and sunk into Justin's chest. She glanced down at his bulging rod and freed herself from his embrace.

"I said someone is knocking on the door. Luckily, it's locked, but I'm, um…" He glanced down at his erection.

She tossed Justin his white coat from the counter as she headed toward the door. "Coming."

She glanced back at Justin, who had put his chef coat back on and pretended to wipe down one of the stoves so his back would be to the door. She glanced down at her hard nipples and grabbed her sweater. Checking to make sure the tag was definitely in the back, she hurriedly threw it over her head and ran her hands through her hair as the knock sounded again.

Upon opening the door, she came face-to-face with one of the students, Bobby, from the class.

"Hey, Ms. Shelbi. I left my book bag over in the corner." Bobby pointed to the black book bag.

"Glad we're still here finishing up." She let the teenager pass into the classroom. Disappointed at the interruption, she was ready to experience the next course Justin wanted to serve.

"Yep, me too. I have a report due tomorrow, and my notes are in here. " He hoisted the book bag up on his shoulder.

Justin walked over with his own belongings and Shelbi's purse and handed it to her.

"Hey, Bobby. We're just leaving. We'll walk out with you." Justin shut off the lights of the classroom and locked the door.

"Relieved I caught you, man. See you next Monday."

Once Bobby left, Justin leaned over and whispered to Shelbi, "It's a good thing I locked the door. I usually don't."

"Because you never had me in there with you before." She winked and proceeded down the hallway in front of him, putting a little extra swish in her walk.

"You know I'm checking you out, don't you?"

"Yep."

"So, where are you going now?"

"Home to cook dinner for my sister Bria." Shelbi checked her watch, wishing she had more time to spend with him, but she didn't. "I promised to make a shrimp bisque tonight. She can't cook, and when I try to teach her, she just doesn't get it, yet she graduated at the top of her class in medical school."

Justin stopped walking and stared at her with a weird expression. She didn't know what she said that would cause such a change in his upbeat spirit of five seconds before.

"What kind of doctor is Bria?" he asked seriously.

Shelbi wasn't sure why the serious shift in their conversation happened. Did he need a doctor perhaps? Was he sick? She knew of six wonderful doctors who could help.

"She's an allergist, but she also focuses on naturopathic options for her patients, such as acupuncture, herbs, or change in diet."

A look of relief washed over his face, and he began walking in step with her again. *Is that the kind of doctor he needs?* She didn't want to ask him. Some people didn't like to feel pressured about going to see a doctor and discussing their medical issues. Besides, she had just met him. Asking about any health issues would seem out of place at such an early stage in their relationship.

He opened the exit door, and she proceeded through it, toward the parking lot.

"I like naturopathic doctors. You never know about those other types of doctors. Patients dying and whatnot and they move on like nothing happened. You know what I mean?"

Shelbi knew exactly what he meant and was glad she didn't blurt out, *"I'm a doctor as well. Oh, and I lost a patient during my internship, which is why I'm a contributing food critic making barely enough to pay my rent or ride the trolley."* She wasn't ready to discuss that part of her life with him yet, or at all, considering she was trying to forget it.

"Well, Bria loves talking about holistic health options and incorporating them with traditional medicine. If you have any

questions or concerns, I'm sure she'd love to speak with you."
There, that way, if he has any health issues, he can ask Bria.

He simply nodded, but his expression held one of worry.

"So, where are you off to?" she asked in order to change the subject. For some reason she felt as if the conversation's tone had changed, and considering he'd just finished driving her crazy up against the refrigerator, she didn't want to lose that high. Plus, she wasn't ready to tell him about her internship or the fact that she was a doctor.

"Picking up my grandmother and bringing her back here for bingo night. She plays every Monday with her girlfriends."

"That's sweet of you."

"She can drive, but not at night. Well, I better get going. She likes to arrive early to get a good spot in the front so she won't miss anything. Thank you so much for assisting me today."

"You're welcome."

He leaned down and kissed her softly on the lips.

"When can I see you again?"

His tone was so serious and direct, her breath escaped her, and she said the first word that came to her mind.

"Tomorrow."

"Cool. I'll be at the restaurant all day and night, but come by and have dinner. Bring Bria since she doesn't cook. Dinner is on the house."

"Cool, we'll be there." She kissed him once more before walking to her car. When she glanced back, his eyes met hers, and he gave her a wink along with a sexy smile. She was in heaven.

*****

"Shelbi, I just feel as if you're wasting your talents."

Shelbi sat in her father's conference room the next morning focused on an abstract painting as if she were having blood drawn from a vein on her arm with a long needle.

That would probably be less painful than sitting in a plush leather chair as my father paces back and forth wearing his white coat with a stethoscope dangling around his neck.

"Dad, I'm not wasting my talents. I'm well qualified to be a food critic. I have my associate's degree in culinary arts, not to mention I started cooking at a young age thanks to Mom and Mother Dear, especially Mother Dear."

"Humph. I should've never moved her in," Dr. Arrington said with a teasing chuckle.

"Daddy, I doubt Mom would want to hear you talk like that about her mother. On another note, I brought you some shrimp bisque, pound cake, and salad for lunch today." She knew the mention of her shrimp bisque and pound cake would shut him up temporarily.

"How many slices of pound cake did you bring?"

"Two, of course. I placed everything in the refrigerator in your office while you examined a patient."

"You can still blog or whatever it's called and practice medicine. It's not too late, Shelbi. I spoke with the chief of medicine at Memphis Central, where you were already accepted to begin your residency program before you decided writing about food was more lucrative. He said you could start your residency in January with the next group of transitional residents."

Her father walked to the head of the table and sat down in his "throne," as her siblings called his chair. He took his reading glasses off his salt-and-pepper hair and handed Shelbi the paperwork she needed to complete in order to begin the residency program.

Shelbi had loved and adored her father since she was a little girl. She admired the way he gave back to his community through his time, discounts, and reasonable payment plans for patients without insurance, and donating money to those less fortunate. He had grown up poor in Hurt Village, an impoverished neighborhood in Memphis, with two siblings and a sick mother. He had watched her work two to three jobs in order to provide for her children. She had been ill for years. With no insurance, poor living conditions, and doctors at the free clinic not really caring about her ailments, Shelbi's grandmother had died from pneumonia, associated with other illnesses, when Dr. Arrington was only sixteen.

"Do you know why I'm a doctor?" he asked seriously.

"Yes, Daddy. You hated how Grandmother Josephine died, and you vowed others in that environment and condition should have doctors caring for them."

She pretended to read over the information about orientation dates, pay schedule, and the letter of commitment—all of which would be shredded and used as cage lining for Bria's pet hamster.

"I think you, Mom, and my siblings are wonderful doctors. You're all compassionate and caring."

"And you think you aren't?"

"I..."

"You've had a very fortunate upbringing, with the best schools, clothes, vacations, and opportunities, so I understand this rebellious attitude you're displaying. You're the youngest, and Sean said that's expected, but it's been almost five months since you graduated from Meharry, and you haven't begun your residency. I know you enjoy the food critic gig. But as a contributing food critic, you aren't making much, even though I assume your personal blog helps out. Do you have medical insurance and retirement benefits?"

Shelbi almost laughed when he mentioned her personal blog. He was totally against her starting it in college because it had nothing to do with medicine and medical schools might have looked at it during the review process.

Shelbi stared straight ahead at another painting. This one had four yellow sunflowers on the canvas. She'd rather be in Raven's examination room with her feet in stirrups. She couldn't blurt out the real reason for not doing her residency. Her dad wouldn't understand.

"Sean also mentioned you may have a fear of failing because you've always been so successful with anything you set your mind to. It's not too late."

Her father continued his lecture, and she tuned him out as she focused on the big picture before her.

Note to self: curse out Dr. Sean Arrington, psychiatrist, middle child, and playboy, before leaving today.

*****

Shelbi waited impatiently in her brother's office while he walked one of Raven's patients to her car. Sean was a flirt and a playboy, even though their father had warned him about flirting with the patients.

She lay down on the chaise lounge meant for his clients, which apparently Sean thought she was one since he'd diagnosed her and shared the information with their father. She'd sue her brother for breach of patient/doctor confidentiality except she wasn't his patient and they'd never discussed her reasons for not completing her residency. But they didn't have to. He was a psychiatrist, for crying out loud, but most importantly, her big brother knew her faults and strengths. Sean had hit the hammer on the nail for part of her reason for not wanting to complete her residency—she was scared to fail. Of course, he didn't know a patient had died under her care and the thought of it happening again was too much to bear.

She closed her eyes for a few moments until the door opened and shut. She opened them to see her brother Sean looking debonair as usual, crashing in his chair in front of her, wearing a black suit and a baby-blue-and-black striped tie over a blue dress shirt. His Hershey chocolate–kissed skin and short, wavy haircut reminded her of a young Blair Underwood, which was why he always had women hanging on tight to him. His six-foot-three frame ruled the office with his commanding presence.

He stretched his Stacy Adams–clad feet out in front of him and picked up his notepad and pencil. "So, um...Dr.

Arrington, what seems to be the problem?" he asked jokingly in a deep professional tone with his pencil poised on the notepad to write her response.

"You're the problem." She crossed her arms over her chest and stared him down like a bull getting ready for the fight.

He nodded and placed his glasses lower on his nose so he could peer over them. He wrote something on the notepad, and Shelbi wrinkled her brow, wondering what on earth he could possibly be writing.

"I see. So why am I the problem?"

"Because you had the audacity to tell Daddy some crap about me being rebellious and not wanting to fail. And what are you writing on the notepad? I'm not a patient."

Sean glanced down at the notepad, gave a wide, devilish grin, and turned it around to show Shelbi. A lady's name and phone number were scribbled on the top line.

"Who's she?"

"The cutie-pie I just walked to the car. I think she could be the future Mrs. Sean...No, wait. What the hell am I saying?"

"Didn't Daddy forbid you to flirt with and date patients?"

"She's Raven's patient; however, I'm available for any counseling she may need, you know what I'm saying?"

"One of Raven's patients?" Shelbi tried not to giggle as she continued. "I don't work here yet, but I know for a fact on Tuesday mornings, Raven doesn't schedule expecting mothers or Pap smears." Shelbi tapped her chin. "You know how organized she is. On Tuesday mornings, Raven only schedules follow-ups for Pap smears—"

"Must you say 'Pap smear' in front of me?"

"Or any possible infections..." Shelbi stopped talking and smirked at her brother.

"What are you trying to say, baby sis?"

"Be careful, big brother. Your player playa days could soon catch up with you. Mom could prescribe some penicillin for you, if need be."

"I'm always careful. Now back to you. Didn't I just hear you say you don't work here *yet*?"

"Um…no." Even though she knew she did. As soon as she said it, she hoped Sean hadn't noticed, but she apparently forgot he was a good listener and dissected everything.

"Unconscious slip, perhaps?" He wrote something on his notepad.

Yep, perhaps.

*****

Shelbi sat in Justin's office the next evening drinking a glass of wine, waiting for him to return from the kitchen. She and Bria had enjoyed their dinner of salmon, whipped white cheddar potatoes, and asparagus.

Her thoughts kept going back to her conversations earlier with her dad and Sean about beginning her residency in a few months. She knew she needed to make a decision soon, but it wasn't easy when she still had guilt lingering over her head.

The office door opened, and Justin walked in with Rasheed trailing behind. He'd offered to keep Bria company while Shelbi hung with Justin. She wasn't sure if that was a good idea considering Rasheed Vincent was a known playboy and always on the gossip blogs with a different woman every week.

"Your sister is hella fine," Rasheed said, sitting on Justin's desk while he grabbed something from the safe.

"Are you being a gentleman with my sister?"

"I'm trying really hard to be," he said as he took an envelope from Justin. "She make a brother wanna turn in his player card."

"Man, stop. You're scaring Shelbi," Justin said. "Where's Bria? You left her by herself?"

"Naw. She's coming. She went to the ladies' room."

The door opened, and Bria walked in. Rasheed hopped off the desk and went straight to her. "Say, you want to go with me upstairs to the bar area and watch the game? I'm off for the rest of the evening, and we can finish our conversation and our bet."

Shelbi looked from Bria to Rasheed and then back to Bria. "What bet?" she asked.

"Stay out of grown folks' business," Rasheed said teasingly to Shelbi before he turned his attention back to Bria, even though his eyes never left her face. He held out his hand. "Such warm, soft hands. Is the rest of your skin this soft and warm?"

"Watch yourself. I'm not the average girlie girl. I can throw you over the banister and have you crashing on the tables below. Don't let my size fool you."

"Damn, she's feisty, too. I like that!" Rasheed ran his tongue over his lips.

"Let's get one thing straight." Bria tapped his chest with her finger and stared up at the six-foot-six man. "I'm not some groupie you've been used to. Now, let's go watch the game so I can win the bet."

"Can I add handcuffs and blindfolds if I win?"

Bria rolled her eyes at him and placed her hand on her hips, wearing a "boy, please" expression on her face. "Do you want to get slapped?"

He grinned devilishly, grabbing her toward him. "Are you adding that if I win?"

"Sure, why not, considering you aren't going to," Bria answered as she walked out with Rasheed following like a stud panting after a female dog in heat.

*****

Once Bria and Rasheed left, Justin and Shelbi settled on the couch talking about absolutely nothing. He let her ramble on about her day visiting a restaurant in Germantown and a meeting with her editor. He didn't care what she discussed. He just wanted to learn more about her and her bubbly personality.

He smiled down at the beautiful woman resting her head against his shoulder, and her arms encircling his waist. He stroked her hair tenderly, kissing her forehead every now and then, which drew pretty smiles on her face or a kiss back on his nose. She was adorable and sexy in a pair of flared jeans and a red halter top that stopped right at her navel, showcasing her flat stomach and a diamond stud in her belly button. But what really got him were the red pumps that he wasn't sure if he wanted to take off and throw across the room or leave on and throw her clothes across the room.

She continued rambling, this time about the restaurant she didn't want to go to the next day and doing some work on her blog. He just wanted to hold her and kiss her supple lips until he needed a bucket of Chap Stick. Her kisses and sweet symphony of moans nearly did him in against the refrigerator the day before. If Bobby hadn't returned for his book bag, Shelbi really may have felt the bulge in his pants up close and personal. The thought of being in her sweet center of paradise made his shaft awaken.

Justin grabbed her and positioned her on his lap so she could feel the bulge he had thanks to her and those damn red heels.

He pulled her to him, kissing her pouty lips, sucking them gently while running his hand along her soft back. He reached one of his hands to the top of her jeans and unbuttoned and unzipped them. She moaned in anticipation and stood to ease the jeans over her luscious hips and thighs, revealing red lacy boy shorts. She stepped out of the jeans, carefully over her shoes, and tossed them to the floor.

"Wow...just wow," he said, admiring her in her heels that accentuated her sexy legs. She sat back on his lap and began to undo his belt buckle. But he had other plans. He flipped her over so she was on her back.

"Jay?"

"Shh, baby. Just lie back and relax. Let Big Daddy do all the work."

"Well, I need to tell you something before you 'get to work,' Big Daddy."

"What's that?" he said, placing kisses down her neck.

"I've only been with one man before."

"Good," he said, still kissing her neck while running a hand over one of her soft legs. He definitely wasn't going to tell her how many women he'd been with. He'd lost count sometime after culinary school.

"One time."

"I heard you." He kissed her on the lips to shush her. He didn't want to hear about some other dude. She stopped kissing him and held his head in her hands, looking up at him with seriousness in her wide doe eyes.

"I mean one guy, only one time. It lasted a minute."

"Oh. I see." *Even better.* "Well, I promise to take things slow with you. We don't have to have sex right now. In fact, that wasn't my intention. Our first time isn't going to be in my office, on my couch, with a restaurant full of customers. However, I wanted to give you a sample of another course."

"Well, proceed on, Big Daddy."

He moved down to the end of the couch and pulled her panties off. He sat on his knees and admired her beautiful trimmed triangle. He rubbed his finger on her rosy bud before replacing it with his tongue, drawing soft moans from her. He sucked and teased it with his tongue, sinking further into the folds of her softness as she spread her legs apart, allowing him more access. He held on to her hips as she started slowly gyrating them while his tongue prodded in and out her. Her hands held on to his head tightly as she shivered and cried out his name over and over. The more she panted and moaned his name, the more he probed deeper into her to give her the pleasure her body begged for.

She raked her fingers through his hair, holding him in place as he licked her ambrosia-filled center. Her breathing became more rapid. Her beautiful breasts heaved up and down as she surrendered herself on his tongue. Her cries and moans mixed in with hints of his name aroused him so much, he had to restrain himself from going any further. He slowly raised himself up and reached out to seize Shelbi in his arms. She came willingly, her breathing still raspy from the orgasm he'd bestowed on her.

"Mmm...you were amazing." She rested her head deeper into his chest and closed her eyes with a sigh of satisfaction.

"I'm glad you enjoyed this course."

"I did, but I think you enjoyed it even more."

CHAPTER SIX

Justin stirred the marinade for the beef ribs for a private party scheduled that evening. B. B. King belted out "Rock Me Baby" while he whistled along. His mind wandered back and forth with thoughts about Shelbi. No matter what he was doing, he couldn't stop thinking about her. A woman had never crowded his brain like Shelbi. Not only had she crowded it, she had practically moved in and taken up most of the space. But he didn't mind. Kissing her supple lips while his hands explored over her dangerous curves was all he could think about. Especially those hips with just enough of a love handle to hold on to while he imagined himself thrusting in and out of her, burying himself into her sweetness until he couldn't hold on any longer. He felt a shudder of the orgasm he hadn't even had yet. He clenched the sides of the prep counter and tried to focus on the task in front of him. He wanted to call her, but she was eating lunch at a restaurant a few doors down that would be featured in her next article. She'd promised to stop by, but he felt impatient and needed to hear her voice.

"What's up, man?"

Rasheed and Derek interrupted Justin's amorous thoughts about Shelbi. He couldn't help it. He wasn't sure how much longer he could wait before making love to her, but he wanted it to be perfect. That wouldn't be hard, because she was perfect.

Rasheed placed a newspaper on the prep counter next to Justin.

Justin carried the marinated ribs to the refrigerator, washed his hands, and hurried back to the newspaper. He knew Shelbi's article had come out today and was anxious to read it.

"Have you read it yet?" Justin asked.

Rasheed pulled a stool from under the prep counter while Derek answered Justin's question.

"Yep. It's good overall." Derek picked up the newspaper and turned to the article. "I mean, four out of five spoons is good."

Justin skimmed through the article, which was laid out in categories: Pros, Cons, Atmosphere, and Interview. While everything else was superior, the cons section wasn't. He read it out loud to Rasheed and Derek, but more so to himself.

"While Lillian's isn't considered to be a barbecue restaurant, patrons can still find barbecue dishes on the menu. However, the owner and executive chef, Justin 'Jay' Richardson, refuses to serve pork because he prefers to offer a healthier approach in the heart of a city widely known for barbecue pork. While his dishes are exemplary, the barbecue sauce was too bland for my taste and needs to be kicked up a notch. Also, the corn bread muffins were a bit too dry and hard, as if they'd been sitting under a heating lamp all day."

Justin threw the newspaper across the prep kitchen and slammed his hand down on the stainless steel counter. How dare she print that! It had never occurred to him she would write a negative review. He assumed she was sharing her thoughts. Now the entire city would think his barbecue sauce was horrible, and to top it all off, the competition was in a few weeks! *What does she know? She's not a chef! She's just a wannabe food expert!*

Derek picked up the newspaper off the floor. "The rest of the article is fine. Just the con section seems sort of bad, but—"

Rasheed cut him off. "Damn, man. I thought you're seeing her. She still cut you down on the barbecue sauce, and the corn bread, too? How you going to sleep with the girl and she give you an awful review? What's the point?"

"I'm seeing her, but not because of the review. And I haven't slept with her yet."

"Well, maybe you should've," Rasheed said sarcastically.

Derek shook his head at Rasheed's comment. "Jay, ignore him. This review isn't going to affect your chances of winning the competition. You've been working on barbecue sauces for a while to compete. One review isn't going to determine whether or not you win."

"I'm going to my office." Justin took the paper from Derek and headed out the door. He needed to be alone.

Justin's cell phone chimed with a text message from Shelbi. *I'm here. Come let me in. The door is locked.*

She was the last person he wanted to see. He couldn't believe she had the audacity to show her face after what she wrote.

He turned around and headed toward the front of the restaurant to let her in, but she was already inside, speaking to one of the servers who'd arrived early at Justin's request to make sure the linens were perfect for the dinner party.

Shelbi's hair was in a bouncy ponytail, and she wore a plaid miniskirt with knee-high boots with the red bottoms. If he weren't upset, he would definitely want to get under her skirt. She flashed him a beautiful smile as if nothing were wrong.

"Hey, Jay. Are you all set for the dinner party?"

He glanced at the waiter, who pretended to double-check tables, even though it was clear he was eavesdropping.

"Just marinated the beef ribs. Let's go to my office." Justin let her pass in front of him.

Once in the office, he closed the door. She reached for him, in an obvious attempt to kiss him, but he sidestepped her and held the newspaper in front of her face.

"What's this?" he asked.

She took the newspaper from him and looked at her article. "This is a good picture of you cutting up onions. I'm glad I sent one of the *Tribune*'s photographers here. He did a good job. There're more pictures on the website. Do you like the article?"

"How are you going to tell me you dislike my barbecue sauce, then put it in the article?"

"Excuse me? What are you talking about?"

"I thought it was between us, Ms. Arrington!"

"There's no such thing as food critic / chef confidentiality!" she sarcastically chastised. "I'm doing my job. Why are you taking this personal?"

"You're kidding me, right?"

She pointed to the article. "This is business. It has nothing to do with us."

"I take my business personally because I built it from the ground up. I worked hard to save and invest my money so I could live my dream using mine and my mother's recipes, including her barbecue sauce. Now thanks to a *contributing* food critic, customers may not patronize my restaurant and I could lose the competition!"

"*Contributing* food critic? And what competition are you referring to?"

"The Pride of Tennessee Barbecue Sauce Competition. I'm entering my barbecue sauce, but thanks to you and your negative comments, I might as well forget it about! You're a food critic. You know they research contestants before the competition. They're probably reading your article now!"

"What? You thought because we're seeing each other I wasn't going to include the cons? Is that why you're seeing me? You're using me!" Shelbi threw the newspaper at him.

"You know that's not true. I've actually been working on other barbecue sauces for you to taste before the competition."

"I'm glad to hear. Now if you'll excuse me, I have another article to write about a *real* barbecue restaurant that serves pork, and their barbecue sauce is to die for. Oh, and the corn bread doesn't taste like Jiffy."

"I'm going to perfect the best barbecue sauce, bottle it, and sell it!"

"Good! Bottle your arrogant, pompous attitude while you're at it, and watch it not sell along with your bland barbecue sauce!" Shelbi slammed the door behind her.

Justin sat at his desk, holding the crumpled newspaper she threw at him, feeling worse than if he'd been slapped. His mother's picture stared at him. Her beautiful smile and caring nature reminded him of Shelbi. The woman he thought could possibly be The One had criticized his barbecue sauce and corn bread. A nervous chuckle escaped him. She called him arrogant and pompous. They were words he never liked. He was a perfectionist. He could deal with that, but arrogant and pompous? He never wanted to come across to anyone with an attitude like that. His mother and grandmother raised him better.

He flicked on the speakers piped through to his office from the main dining area. B. B. King's "The Thrill is Gone" sounded through. He rested his head on the high-back swivel chair, closing his eyes.

"Yep, the thrill is gone."

*****

Shelbi sat on her bed reading over the draft she'd written on the barbecue restaurant from earlier in the day. She had made several errors and at one point called the restaurant by the wrong name. She hit backspace on the keyboard, became frustrated, closed the laptop, and pushed it under the bed.

Working hadn't reduced her thoughts about her argument with Justin as she had hoped. Did he actually think she would leave that tidbit of information out because they had been spending time together?

She thought he was different. She thought she had found the man she could easily introduce to her family and they would welcome him into their home. Well, maybe not Cannon and Sean at first, but once they realized what a terrific guy he was—or she thought he was—they would've invited him for a round of golf or to a Memphis Grizzlies game. But he'd shown his true colors today. He was arrogant, conceited, and didn't take criticism very well. One can't be a perfectionist and not expect to have some kind of failure.

Wait…no. My situation is different.

Bria's pet hamster rustled on his paper, mostly Shelbi's shredded residency information. She was hamster sitting since Bria was out of town for the next few days at a holistic medical convention and had insisted he stay with Shelbi so she could keep the hamster company.

"What am I going to do, Mr. Hamster?" Shelbi went over to his cage. He was having a late-night snack of sunflower seeds. "If someone doesn't like my cooking, I improve it, not go off on them, but cooking isn't my life. It's Justin's. It's his calling."

She stooped down in front of the dresser where the hamster continued to nibble on his food.

"He has to be a perfectionist, or customers won't patronize. But it was my opinion. I needed a little more oomph in the sauce. Others may not care. Right? I'm glad he's working on another one, though. Too bad I'll never taste it."

Shelbi sighed and walked away from the hamster. Apparently bored of her rambling, he chose to curl up and drift off to sleep. It was ten minutes to eleven, and she needed to do the same, except she knew rest wasn't going to come easily tonight.

Her cell phone rang from the nightstand. She checked the screen, surprised to see Justin's name.

"Hello?"

"I'm downstairs by the Amtrak station. Can I come speak to you for a moment?"

Moments later, he stood at her door wearing his black-and-white checked chef's pants and his white chef jacket stained with red splashes. He carried a medium-sized box. She allowed him in, but didn't speak. Instead, she sat on the couch, and he joined her on the other end.

"I have something for you." He carefully handed her the box. She set it on the coffee table in front of her and opened it to see six jars.

"What's all this?"

"I made five different barbecue sauces for you to sample. I've been working on them since I met you on the trolley and you told me my signature sauce was bland. The sixth bottle is for you." He took an empty bottle out of the box and handed it to her. There was a computer-printed label on it that read: *Justin's Arrogant and Pompous Attitude.*

Shelbi laughed as she read the bottle. "You're something else, you know?"

"I know, and I apologize. If you think I should bottle my arrogant and pompous attitude, then I will. I'm sorry for snapping at you earlier. I need to learn to take criticism. I'm a perfectionist. These are the barbecue sauces I have created for the competition. I have to enter three different flavors. I did alter the one you said is bland. I would like your honest opinion on all of them."

"I noticed they're all on your jacket."

"Shelbi, I'm not seeing you because I was trying to get a good review. I'm sorry you felt that way, and I'm sorry I made it seem as if your opinion didn't matter or count because you're a contributing food critic and not the head food critic. I hope we can start over again fresh." He scooted closer to her on the couch, and she smelled a hint of his breathtaking cologne that hadn't been smothered by all of the barbecue sauce he made.

She picked up one of the bottles from the box and was pleasantly surprised by the label. "Shelbi's Kick It Up a Notch Barbecue Sauce." She smiled and leaned over to kiss him tenderly on the lips.

"Now it's hot and spicy, like you."

"Kiss me again," she whispered.

And he obliged.

CHAPTER SEVEN

Shelbi waited impatiently for Justin to arrive at her apartment so they could eat a late- night dinner together. She didn't understand how he could work all day at his restaurant and still want to cook again with her. They had spent practically all of their free time together preparing meals, kissing, going to the movies and dance clubs, and falling for each other over the past few weeks. Shelbi was giddy with delight at the notion of seeing him. She thought he would tire of spending time with her, but he hadn't.

The idea of him arriving at her door at any moment brought a wide smile to her lips. She couldn't remember the last time she was so excited about a man coming over.

Justin made her feel, say, and desire things she had never experienced before. Lust. Need. Sex. The thought of him made her breath catch in her throat and caused a warm, throbbing ache between her legs only Justin could satisfy.

As the doorbell chimed, happy flutters in her stomach danced. She bounced off the couch so fast, tossed her *Bon Appétit* magazine in the air, and stumbled over the coffee table. She checked her hair in the mirror by the door and peeked out the peephole just to make sure it was him. She opened the door and showered him with kisses all over his face.

"Miss me?" He grinned sleepily.

She stood back and looked up at him. She placed one hand over her heart and the other on his cheek, shaking her head in concern.

"Jay, you look so tired. You could've gone home."

"Nonsense. I love being and cooking with you. Smells like you already started." He moved toward the kitchen and lifted the lid off the pot on the stove.

"I made the red beans, rice, and corn bread. I didn't sauté the sausage yet because you said you'd rather do it, but I cut up everything for you." She pointed to the cutting board where the beef sausage, onions, and bell peppers were already diced.

"Thanks. But I like a little more onion. Have another one?"

Shelbi reached into the refrigerator. "Yep. I'll cut it for you. Go sit down and relax. You've been on your feet all day." She smiled to herself because she remembered plenty of times when her mother had said a similar line to her father after he came home from a long day. Her mother had been a stay-at-home mom until Shelbi entered first grade.

She raked the ingredients she cut into a mixing bowl and placed the onion on the cutting board next to the knife.

Justin playfully bumped her out of the way with his hip and swatted her butt. "Let Big Daddy handle this," he said, grabbing her in his arms and stooping down to eye level to give her a deep, tender kiss. "You've done everything else. I brought you some dessert. Grab the bag I set on the foyer table."

"Is it Memphis mud pie?" She jumped up and down in his arms. She had been begging him to make her one for over a week.

"You'll just have to go see." He kissed her again, and she rubbed her nose on his before leaving his warm embrace.

She skipped over to the foyer table and happily retrieved the pie.

Shelbi felt lucky to find a warm, chivalrous, and sexy man like Justin. She loved the way he held her, kissed her, and made her feel as if she were the only woman in his world. He genuinely cared about her well-being and actually listened to what she said, even when she thought he wasn't listening. She loved the picnic they had at the park a few days ago. They had lain on the blanket, shooting the breeze about absolutely nothing as she rested her head on his chest and he tenderly stroked her hair. She couldn't remember a more peaceful time before that moment. She had never felt so in sync with a man.

"Jay, this looks scrumptious," she said, returning to the kitchen with the pie and setting it in the refrigerator.

He looked up from chopping the onion with a sleepy smile on his face. "Thank you, bab...ow...crap..." Justin yelled out.

Shelbi looked down at his finger to see blood spewing from it. She immediately grabbed a clean dish towel from the drawer and wrapped the bleeding finger.

"Raise your arm a little more and apply direct pressure on the cut so the bleeding will stop. I'll go get my first aid kit." Shelbi took off upstairs to grab her first aid kit from her closet.

"Shelbi, I'm fine. Just bring a bandage."

"Nonsense," she called out, rushing back downstairs with the kit tucked under her arm as she put on plastic gloves. She led him to the sink and removed the dish towel to let the cool water run over the cut. She lifted his finger to examine it before placing it back under the water. She threw away the onion he was cutting, tossed the knife into the other sink, and poured a few capfuls of bleach over it. She examined his finger once more.

"It's deep. It needs more than a bandage. I can stitch it for you. I'll call Bria. She may have some pain—"

Justin jerked his head toward her and snatched his finger away as if she had said she was going to cut it off.

"Shelbi, wait! How do you know how to stitch up a cut?"

"My sister taught me," Shelbi answered with a nonchalant shrug, referring to Raven.

"Okay, I'll feel more comfortable if Bria does it, since she apparently knows how."

"Boy, please, I've been stitching up cuts since I was a teenager. But I'll call Bria if it makes you feel better. You just keep that finger under the running water, mister."

Shelbi picked up her cell phone to call Bria, who didn't answer until the fifth ring.

"What?" Bria answered in a low tone, yet she seemed wide awake.

"Well, hello, sunshine. What a warm welcome."

"Girl, it's almost midnight. What's wrong?"

"You've called me much later when you've had the midnight munchies. Anyway, Jay cut his finger, so I'm going to stitch it in a moment, but I called to see if you had some pain medicine samples lying around or something to numb the finger so he won't feel the pain."

"Okay, I'll set it outside the door in a minute."

"Not safe, Dr. Bria. Bring it to me."

Long, silent pause.

"Humph. Fine, I'll see you in a minute."

Shelbi thought their conversation strange. First of all, Bria would never set medicine outside of the door, and second, she would've automatically volunteered to stitch the cut herself. *Hmm.* Bria's mouth dripped like a leaky faucet when it came to whom she was dating, so Shelbi doubted she had company. Bria always asked for her opinion. Maybe she was just tired.

*****

Ten minutes later, Shelbi was stitching up Justin's cut with Bria looking on, holding a flashlight over his finger for extra light. At first, he wanted Bria to sew the stitch since she was a doctor, but when Bria confirmed Shelbi definitely knew how, he didn't want anyone else but Shelbi to tend to him.

He really appreciated Shelbi's quick and calm thinking. Most women would've freaked out if they saw blood gushing from his finger, but not his Shelbi. Her caring nature reminded him of his mother. She never panicked when her children had scrapes, cuts, or broken limbs. She tended to him and Reagan in a loving and calm manner, just as Shelbi had done, and he knew she would be the same with their own children. Thinking about having children with Shelbi surprised him. He knew he wanted a family someday, but he could actually visualize it with her.

Justin tried not to watch as the needle and thread—which Bria called surgical suture—went in and out of his finger. Shelbi had applied some type of numbing agent to the area so he wouldn't feel the pain, but he still didn't want to watch. Instead, he put his focus on something else, as Shelbi had suggested before she began. He stared at a crystal Ferris wheel on her bookshelf, but every now and then, he would glance at her serious and intense facial expression. Her sewing of the stitch was precise. She concentrated on the task at hand, and he was impressed by this side of her.

When Shelbi was finished, she disposed of her gloves and washed her hands while Bria inspected the stitches

"Good work, Dr. Shelbi. Justin, I'm going to give you the name and number of a doctor friend of mine. He can look at this for you in a few days to make sure it doesn't become infected. His name is Dr. Braxton. He's a general family doctor a few blocks up from here, not far from St. Jude's Hospital. I'll send him a text in a few to let him know."

"Cool. Anything else?" he asked.

"Keep it dry for the next few days. And the medicine you took should kick in within a few minutes, just so you want have any discomforting pain tonight, but I wouldn't drive home, and the trolley has already stopped running."

"Thank you, Bria, for the information. I'll give him a call in the morning." *Maybe.*

Bria scribbled the information on the piece of paper Shelbi handed her. Justin looked at her handwriting.

He grinned. "Doctors sure do write sloppy. Of course, it doesn't explain why Shelbi writes sloppy." He placed the slip of paper in his wallet and walked toward the kitchen to finish cooking.

"Well, Shelbi is a—"

"Is a mess when it comes to writing. I've been writing sloppy since I was child. Just never learned how to write neat. I prefer to type whenever possible. Bria, it's getting late, sweetie, and you have to get up early in the morning to get your hair done. I'll walk you out."

"Wait a minute. What are you cooking that smells so yummy?" Bria walked into the kitchen, where Justin was sautéing the ingredients Shelbi had cut up earlier.

"Red beans and rice."

"I have to stay and have a taste."

Shelbi walked over to the cabinet and grabbed a bowl and foil from a drawer. "I'll make it to go for you, sis."

Justin wondered why Shelbi was acting so strange and wanted to rush her sister out.

"Cool. Can you make two bowls for me? You know how greedy I am," Bria said.

After Bria left with her hearty portions of red beans and rice, Justin and Shelbi sat on the floor around her coffee table, with their backs against the bottom of the sofa, since she didn't own a dining set yet. He was feeling dizzy from the medicine. He was already sleepy when he arrived, but now he wanted to cuddle next to Shelbi in her bed and go to sleep.

"Baby, I have to admit, I was kind of surprised you knew how to actually stitch up a cut. I'm impressed. What other talents do you have besides throwing down on these red beans and rice?" He took his last bite and guzzled the rest of his water.

"Hmm…well, I'm a…" Her voice trailed off.

"You're a what?" he asked curiously.

She seemed to contemplate over something. She gulped down the rest of her wine and closed her eyes for a moment before looking at him.

"I'm a...an avid reader, I can cook, play the clarinet, and play pool."

"Yeah right. You can really play pool?"

"Why does that surprise you? I have two older brothers. But Bria is really the athletic, sporty one."

"Hmm...my boy really digs her. She was at the restaurant tonight watching the game with some fellas while Rasheed was working."

"Oh really? Yeah, she is definitely the family tomboy. She can play basketball, tennis, volleyball, and softball. Growing up, she always hung around the boys, but she's still a girlie girl. Most of her friends are men. I guess she has added Rasheed to her list."

"You mean like friends with benefits?" he asked curiously. That would be right up Rasheed's alley.

"Oh, nothing like that. She hasn't and won't sleep with any of them. She's celibate."

Well damn. I guess my boy can forget about hooking up with her.

Justin let out a long, wide yawn and rested his head on Shelbi's shoulder. She kissed his forehead tenderly, and he nuzzled up even closer. Lying on her was warm and relaxing. The medicine had officially kicked in. The pain was gone, and he began to find himself slowly drifting off to sleep, lowering his head on her breasts. They were the best pillows he had ever lain on. A slight, gentle knock on his forehead caused him to jerk his eyes open to find her smiling sleepily at him.

"Go upstairs, take a shower, and climb in the bed. I'll be up in a minute, after I clean up down here."

"Thank you for taking care of me. You're an amazing woman, Shelbi Arrington." He kissed her gently on the lips, becoming dizzy as she caressed his lips with hers. A realization transpired over him. He was feeling...weird. No, not weird. Calm? A newfound feeling, but it wasn't really new at all. He had felt it when he first met her, but didn't know how to explain it. Maybe it was her attention to the cut, cuddling with her on the floor, her cooking, or the fact she could play pool.

Okay, I'm delirious. Just because she can play pool doesn't mean I'm falling in love with her. Could it? Naw. It's this damn medicine.

Despite the fuzzy haze clouding his thoughts, he remained coherent enough to recognize he wanted to make love to her. He needed to feel her naked body under his while he buried himself deep inside her sweet body. Hear her sweet moans as she held on to him, gripping his back and taking his full length deeper inside her until she exploded her nectar around him.

She knocked her soft knuckle on his forehead again, and he slowly opened his eyes to see the beautiful angel before him.

"Jay, you fell asleep kissing me." She laughed. "Poor thing. How about you skip the shower and I help you upstairs?"

He was too weak to argue. Even though he wanted to make love to her, tonight wouldn't be the time. He needed to be alert and have all of his strength to satisfy her over and over and over.

"Okay, help me upstairs."

And that was the last thing he remembered saying before his head hit the pillow.

*****

Shelbi stared at the digital clock on her nightstand. It was seven in the morning. Justin's arms had remained around her as they spooned together all night. His soft snoring finally lulled her to sleep after she stayed awake for an hour trying to figure out what on earth he mumbled after she said good night to him. It sounded like...no. He couldn't possibly have said those words. She couldn't make out all of them. Just one. *Love*.

Maybe he had said he loved the red beans and rice or the goose-down comforter.

He stirred gently behind her, and a tender kiss to the back of her neck sent a soft sigh from her throat. The hard wall of his chest was comforting against her back, and she wished it wasn't time to rise.

"Good morning, beautiful." His morning voice was gruff yet sexy.

She smiled. It was nice to wake up next to him. It was the first time they had ever spent the night together.

"You may not think so once I turn around."

"Hmm...I doubt it." He kissed her neck again, sending a jolt through her as if she had just been Tasered. "Thank you again for stitching up my cut. I promise to not get it wet."

"Please don't, and call Dr. Braxton. I know him as well. He's a good doctor." He'd graduated from medical school with Sean. He and Bria had gone on a few dates, but she wasn't interested in him.

"We'll see." He sat all the way up in the bed and propped the pillows behind his back. She turned over and rested her head on his bare chest, making circles around the tattoo of the heart with his mother's name inside of it.

Shelbi noticed the casualness of his words, as if he didn't care about going to a doctor at all. "You don't have to go to him. It's just a suggestion. You can go to your own doctor."

"I don't have a doctor. I really don't like going to them."

Oh great. He's one of those men who thinks he's too strong of a man to go to a doctor.

"Why not?"

"Baby, I gotta go," he said abruptly in an annoyed tone. He pushed the comforter off him and sat on the edge of the bed.

She didn't understand what she had said to set him off.

"Is there something wrong, Jay?"

"No. I have a staff meeting at nine, and I have to run home first."

"Too bad. I was going to make you breakfast."

He turned and kissed her on her forehead, running a finger down her cheek. "I would've loved for you to cook breakfast, but one Saturday a month, Rasheed, Derek, and I meet with the entire staff. The sous chef and the line cooks cook breakfast.

They should be there now." Justin glanced at the clock. He jumped out of the bed and pulled on his pants. "I'll call you later on today. I have a full day. A jazz band is coming to set up for tonight and rehearse around noon. I promised to make catfish and hush puppies with sweet potato fries for lunch for them. What are you doing today?" He threw on his shirt and slipped his feet into his loafers.

"I'm having lunch with my sisters at Rendezvous, and then we're going shopping at Wolfchase Galleria."

"Cool. Will you stop by the restaurant tonight? The band plays their first set at seven."

"Sure. I'll see if my sisters want to come."

"Great. Thank you for taking care of me last night." He leaned over and kissed her one more time on the forehead before running down the stairs.

*****

Justin rode the trolley home, leaving his Navigator at Shelbi's apartment building. The grogginess of the medicine hadn't worn off yet. His hand didn't hurt anymore, but it was itching under the gauze, annoying the heck out of him.

He wasn't sure about going to see the doctor Bria suggested. His hate for doctors had waned somewhat over the years, depending on the type of medicine they practiced. He tolerated allergists like Bria. General doctors, or worse, a surgeon like the asshole who didn't save his mother, weren't on his top ten list of doctors. It brought up too many painful memories and the thought of losing his mother at the hands of a young surgeon who seemed more interested in rushing out to a party.

Justin remembered the last time he saw the surgeon—his mother's funeral. He was surprised the man had shown up pretending to be sad. When the doctor had paid his respects, he told Justin he understood his pain, for he had lost his mother at a young age as well. He even told Justin if he needed anything, all he had to do was call.

Justin had become angry and screamed out, *"You killed my mother!"* during the funeral. His grandmother had taken him out into the hallway to scold him, but he didn't want to hear anything she had to say. He just wanted to lie on his mother's chest and cry.

Justin hadn't meant to cut Shelbi off and leave abruptly. He could've stayed for breakfast and still made it to the restaurant on time. He just didn't feel like going into detail about his dislike for doctors so early in the freaking morning. He would tell her once he was comfortable to talk about his mother's death with her.

Right now his focus was on the barbecue competition tomorrow. He had taken Shelbi's advice into consideration and was going to enter the brown sugar, the caliente, and his signature sauce, which was now her favorite. He already had a dozen of each bottled, boxed, and locked in his office. The competition was a way to promote more business for his restaurant, even if he didn't win. Regardless of winning, which he hoped he would, Derek was already in the process of working on having the barbecue sauces sold in the restaurant's gift shop, where they already sold T-shirts, shot glasses, and other souvenirs the patrons, mostly tourists, bought.

Shelbi planned to attend the competition to support him and write an article for her personal blog. He realized it wasn't the medicine or sleepiness last night that made him think he was falling in love with Shelbi. It has her attentiveness to him, her sweet smile, which lit up his world, the way she carried herself like a lady, and her sassy attitude. He knew without a doubt he was falling in love with her and he wasn't going to ever let her go. He wanted her, and soon she would know just how much.

CHAPTER EIGHT

"So, what's going on with you?" Raven asked.

Shelbi sat in a booth across from her sisters at Rendezvous barbecue restaurant. She tried to concentrate on the menu, but their inquiring stares began to annoy her. She took a sip of her water with lemon, hoping she was imagining their inquisitive gazes. However, when Raven spoke wearing a slightly sarcastic facial expression and pursed her lips together at the end of the question, waiting for the answer, she wanted a real answer and not just an "oh, nothing much" answer. Raven wanted to know what was really going on, and be given all the details, including time, date, and what outfit you wore, if it was important to the answer. Sometimes, Shelbi wondered why Raven didn't decide to become a detective the way she interrogated people to get the information she wanted.

"Oh, nothing much," Shelbi answered. She continued to stare at the menu until Raven snatched it from her.

Raven smacked her lips together. "Chile, please. And why are you studying the menu? We always order the pulled pork nachos for the appetizer, and you always order the beef brisket sandwich."

"Hmm. Can we order the chicken nachos instead? I'm trying to cut down on my pork intake."

"What? Since when have you cared about that? Where's our favorite waiter?" Raven asked, looking around for the waiter they had requested. He'd been waiting tables at Rendezvous for over twenty years. The Arrington family requested only him when they dined there.

Shelbi glanced at Bria because she knew her sister was about to put her two cents into the conversation.

"You know she's seeing the healthy chef over at Lillian's. He doesn't serve pork. She made some red beans and rice last night with beef sausage, not andouille. It was still good, but…"

"Hmm…the healthy chef?" Raven asked. "I like his restaurant. We could've gone there for lunch."

Shelbi shook her head. "He's not open for lunch on Saturdays and Sundays, but he did invite us to come out tonight. Are you ladies game?"

Bria looked up from her menu. "I was already going. Rasheed invited me to hang, but I think Raven is on baby alert."

Raven nodded and glanced at her cell phone. "I have a patient that may deliver tonight, so I'll have to take a rain check."

Shelbi worried about Raven often and tried to get her out of the house and the rut she was in. She had placed all of her focus on her career ever since her husband died a year ago, in the line of duty on the Memphis police force, just three months after their wedding.

Their favorite waiter came to take their order. Raven and Bria decided they would try the chicken nachos. They also ordered a pitcher of beer and made Raven the designated driver.

Shelbi turned her focus on Bria. "So, are you interested in Rasheed? Jay says he really likes you." Shelbi hoped to take the focus of today's conversation off of her.

"Girl, no. We're just friends. But I have a question for you." Bria poured two glasses of beer from the pitcher the waiter dropped off, while Raven sipped on iced tea.

Here it comes, the same ole conversation.

"Last night you cut me off and practically kicked me out when I tried to tell Jay you're a doctor too. Doesn't he know?"

Okay, a new conversation.

"No."

"Are you going to tell him? I mean, doesn't he find it weird you know how to stitch up a cut?"

"Nope, I told him my sister taught me, and then when you confirmed I knew how, he was fine."

"But I assumed he knew you were a doctor. What are you scared of? Last night clearly showed you knew what to do." Bria stopped talking as the waiter brought their barbecue chicken nachos and three plates.

Shelbi found Raven's eyes on her again, brooding over something as usual. Raven pulled her thick, naturally curly hair into a ponytail on top of her head. Her long hair always got caught in her mouth while she ate. But instead of digging into the nachos, she rested her hands on the table and stared at Shelbi with a concerned face. Raven was the oldest sister, but not the oldest child, having been born five minutes after Cannon. Even though they were twins, he still took the role of the oldest child very seriously, as did Raven, when it came to her sisters. She spoke quietly when addressing Shelbi.

"What are you scared of? Did something happen during your internship you aren't telling us about?"

Shelbi lowered her gaze to the table. Her emotions were torn. Last night, when Justin had cut himself, she acted on instinct as soon as the blood gushed from his finger. Her adrenaline had been running in overtime, and she hadn't come down yet. It made her miss seeing patients at the hospital and being in the environment of making people feel better. Unfortunately, that wasn't always possible, which scared her the most.

Shelbi took a deep breath, a swig of her beer, and looked across the table at her sisters. They gave her their undivided attention.

"During my internship, my group was assigned a patient per intern to watch over and care for during rounds under Dr. Clouse, my attending doctor."

Raven nodded. "Mmm…I know Dr. Clouse. He's such a hothead. I'm glad I had another attending during my internship in medical school."

"Anyway, one day I noticed my patient, Sam, didn't look so hot. I checked out his symptoms, which were similar to a disease I had written a paper on a few weeks before. I pointed it out to Dr. Clouse, who said I was incorrect. He said I was only in medical school and not a doctor yet and I wasn't allowed to diagnose anything."

Bria shook her head. "Sis, that happens all the time. Even if you were correct, attending physicians couldn't care less what an intern has to say."

"I was correct, but when he brushed me off, I thought perhaps he was right. I mean, I was still in medical school, and he was a doctor. Afterwards, Dr. Clouse diagnosed Sam with something else and began treatments, but he wasn't getting any better. Dr. Clouse did some more research with one of the residents and realized I was correct. He tried to give Sam the proper treatments, but it was too late. Sam died a few days later." She wiped the tears from eyes. "I could've done more, but I didn't."

Raven reached over the table and placed a comforting hand over Shelbi's. "Baby sis, you couldn't do anything about that. Sam wasn't your patient, and sometimes attending physicians aren't going to listen to interns, or even residents, for that matter. Sweetie, I know you. You aren't a quitter or a failure. It's sad when a patient dies and you feel you could've done more."

"And that's another issue I have. How can you just move on and not feel any remorse? During my internship, I saw doctors just walking out the door laughing, and so soon after telling someone their loved one just died."

"Shelbi, we've all been there. It hurts, but we have to move on. Trust me, I betcha Dr. Clouse felt like crap afterwards. I've seen our parents hurting after patients die. Just last month, I delivered a stillborn baby. It's the saddest thing to witness, but we have to accept we can't save everyone. If we carry it with us wherever we go and stay depressed, we won't be effective doctors for other patients."

The waiter returned with their entrées and another pitcher of beer.

"But do you know, the best thing about being a doctor," Raven continued once the waiter left, "is seeing the patients get better and knowing you had a hand in it. In my case, I love to see the delight on the parents' faces that had trouble conceiving, only to deliver a healthy baby. It's an amazing joy."

"Daddy said he gave you the information packet from Memphis Central Hospital. It's not too late," Bria said.

"Umm...I kind of put it through the shredder, and then I placed it in Mr. Hamster's cage when I hamster sat."

Her sisters laughed, and Shelbi smiled, feeling a little better.

They ate their food quietly for a few minutes. Shelbi thought about what Raven had said, but she wasn't sure if she was ready to return. She was enjoying her gig as a food critic, but she missed caring for patients as well. Taking care of Justin's cut had reminded her of why she wanted to be a doctor in the first place.

Bria tilted her head to the side and laid confused eyes on Shelbi. "I still don't understand why you haven't told Justin you're a doctor."

"I'm not ready to share that information yet without having to go into grave detail as to why I'm not doing my residency. I barely wanted to tell you two, and you're my sisters. As of right now, I don't know what I'm going to do. So I would appreciate if this conversation stays among the three of us until I make up my mind. That includes not telling our parents or brothers. You know Sean has already analyzed me. Right now, I just want to enjoy my beef brisket sandwich and coleslaw."

Her sisters promised. Shelbi's phone beeped, and a text message from Jay made her smile.

Miss you, baby. It felt good to hold you last night.

"Must be the healthy chef saying something dirty because your face is turning red," Raven said.

"No. Get your mind out of the gutter."

"Oh, tell him I spoke to Dr. Braxton earlier, and he said Jay can come at seven on Monday morning. He'll be there catching up on paperwork," Raven said before biting into a rib and licking her fingers.

Shelbi typed Bria's message into the cell phone and placed it on the table to wait for his response. The phone beeped with his message.

I'll see. Gotta go fry some catfish now. See you tonight.

Shelbi sighed. Every time she mentioned he should go to see a doctor, he acted indifferent. He must be scared, which was understandable. Doctors didn't always deliver the best news, but he was only going to get his stitches taken out, not his appendix. She decided to text him back before he started on the catfish.

Jay, you're having a few stitches removed, not your appendix! LOL! XOXO.

Once the ladies were done, they headed out to Wolfchase Galleria mall in Germantown with Raven driving. Shelbi sat in the backseat of Raven's Mercedes checking her cell phone for a reply text message from Jay. She figured he was busy preparing the lunch for the jazz band and tossed her phone into her purse.

She would give some careful thought and consideration about starting her residency, but she didn't want to be forced. She knew, when and if the time was right, she would continue her medical career.

CHAPTER NINE

Shelbi and Bria sat jamming to the jazz trio playing an original, upbeat piece. The restaurant was extremely busy. The sous chef, who was originally off, had been called in to assist Justin. Shelbi was slightly disappointed Justin couldn't walk the floor tonight, but he was the executive chef, and she understood. She had spoken to him briefly when he brought out their dinner. He had to hurry back to the kitchen, but not before he placed a deep kiss on her lips. The envious eyes of other women followed him back to the kitchen after the gesture, probably wishing they were in her Louboutins. *Sorry, girls, he's mine.*

The restaurant was crowded, and the wait was forty-five minutes. Couples on dates, ladies hanging with their girls, and men hanging with their boys comprised the usual Saturday night crowd at Lillian's. Shelbi and Bria were fortunate Rasheed had already reserved a table for them in the VIP section near the stage so they could enjoy the show.

Shelbi watched Bria's eyes follow Rasheed as he walked around to check on the guests. He was quite professional, but every now and then, she caught him throwing his smooth, suave charm on some chick giggling her heart out over something the handsome retired basketball player said. To her surprise, when Rasheed flirted with a table of gorgeous model-looking women, Bria didn't flinch. If it had been Justin, Shelbi would've been upset, but Bria sat contentedly, sipping her frozen margarita and nibbling on crab cakes as she bobbed her head to the jazz.

"Bria..." Shelbi paused, deciding to chew the rest of her salmon. "Watching Rasheed flirt with other girls doesn't bother you?"

Bria shot her an annoyed look and sipped her drink. She had been celibate for almost two years since her fiancé got another woman pregnant, yet wanted to be forgiven and get married as planned. She had thrown the ring into the Mississippi River and never looked back.

"Girl, no," Bria groaned. "We're just friends. Do I need to spell it for you? F—"

"Don't get smart. I just thought there was something more between you two. You guys looked rather cozy when you first met."

"He's a cool guy, but he's such a player. Been there, done that. Besides, he calls me for advice about his different honeys. Why would I want to date him?" Bria glanced in his direction. Rasheed smiled and nodded his head toward a pretty girl with a long weave and a low-cut dress. "See? He wants my approval now." Bria shook her head in the negative at the girl he pointed out.

"Why did you shake her head at her? She's cute."

"Mmm...yeah...but not his type."

Shelbi laughed. "Really? You've known him a few weeks, but you already know his type?"

"Yep." Bria nodded and turned her focus on the band.

"Was he at your place when I called you last night?"

"Yeah. We watched some TV and hung for a while until he got a call from some of his basketball buddies about going to the strip club. He liked your red beans and rice, by the way."

"I was wondering why you asked for two big bowls."

Shelbi's cell phone vibrated next to her plate. She had a text from Jay.

Meet me in my office.

Shelbi's knees turned to jelly and her breath caught in her throat at his command, yet she still stood quickly to obey his request.

She downed the rest of her amaretto sour. "I'll be back."

A few moments later, Shelbi's lips met Justin's as he pressed her back against the door. She'd barely closed and locked it before he grabbed her hard to him. She tossed his chef's hat on the floor so she could run her fingers through his wild hair. His hands gripped her face as if he just couldn't get enough of her, devouring her lips aggressively like a sailor returning home from being out to sea for six months. His lips left hers and moved down to her throat before he turned her around so her back lay against his rock-hard chest. His hard bulge rubbed against her butt, and she placed her hands on the door to steady herself as he kissed her neck and kneaded her breasts hard.

"I want to be inside you so bad." He ran his hand up her short black dress until he found her wet center, waiting for him. He rubbed the rosy knob, inducing sounds of pleasure from her. One finger slid into her, going in and out of the slippery vessel, making her wish it was his throbbing erection. She rubbed her butt on his hard shaft as an invitation.

"I want you now too, Jay. Please! Please!" She banged her fist on the door. Her begging and pleading was out of character for her, but she didn't care. Her emotions were turned all the way up to sex, lust, and pleasure. She had to have him now, right now, in his office despite the fact there was a restaurant full of customers.

"Not here, baby." He kissed her neck tenderly. "Not in my office, not for our first time."

She could barely stand up much longer. Her knees buckled, and she tried not to scream out as she had an orgasm. He removed his lips from her neck and placed them on hers to smother her cry of ecstasy.

Moments later, she sat on his lap, resting her head on his chest, tracing the outline of his name stitched in a bold dark blue thread. She needed to cool down after her intoxicating orgasm. He had to go back to the kitchen in a few minutes. He'd told his sous chef he needed a twenty-minute break, and they had a few more moments.

"Jay, I'm excited about the competition tomorrow."

"Me too. This could be it. Plus, you'll be by my side, and that's very important to me."

"Really?" she asked in a shocked manner.

Justin was the first man to ever make her feel special and needed. The men she had dated in the past had never wanted to take the time to get to know her, which had turned her off considerably. After all the begging she had just done with Justin, he still would rather wait until the proper time to make love to her. She smiled and kissed him lightly on the lips.

"Shelbi, you're very important to me." His voice and eyes held so much warmth and compassion, she couldn't help but let out a long sigh of relief. She'd finally found The One. She lifted his hand to her lips and kissed it, remembering his cut finger. She took the safety pin out of the gauze to unwrap it and examine the stitches. They looked pretty good, but he still needed to go see a doctor. She rewrapped it quickly because he had to leave in a moment.

"Speaking of very important, make sure you go see Dr. Braxton on Monday."

"Shelbi…" he started and then abruptly took her off his lap and set her on the couch. He walked to his desk, looking for something, obviously avoiding the conversation as he'd done that morning.

"What's the problem, Jay? I'm not telling you to go get a physical. You need to have it checked just to be on the safe side. I did stitches at my apartment! It can become infected. Do you want your finger to fall off?"

"Shelbi, you don't understand." He picked up his chef's hat from the floor and strode toward the door.

She rose and moved quickly to stand in front of him. She was tired of him avoiding the conversation and figured she needed to know the reason he didn't want to go to the doctor so she could be supportive and encourage him otherwise.

"I don't understand what? I know plenty of people who are scared of going to doctors. I don't like going to them either. It's scary. You don't know what they're going to say or do. Oh, and don't get me started on having blood work done. I have the craziest veins, and the nurses can never find them. But Jay, you'll be fine."

"Shelbi…" he sighed, looking away toward his desk and then back down to her.

"I'll go with you," she said in a sincere tone, placing her hands on his waist and drawing him closer. She wrapped her arms tightly around him. She had never seen such a strained look on his face. It had crumpled and then turned into a "please stop pestering me" expression.

"Fine, I'll go, but only because it's important to you. Plus, I need my finger since you swear it's going to fall off. I gotta get back to the kitchen." He kissed her on the forehead, and they headed out of the office.

Shelbi passed the employees ladies' room on the way back to the dining room. She had no idea if she looked disheveled or not after the passionate episode in Justin's office. Upon entering the ladies' room, she saw Brooklyn bending over the sink, washing her hands. A flushed face and sunken eyes alerted Shelbi that Brooklyn wasn't well. She took deep breaths and exhaled to help ease the pain she was obviously feeling. A bottle of medicine was sitting on the counter next to her purse.

"Brooklyn, are you okay?" she asked, rubbing her back.

"Shelbi, I don't know what's wrong with me," Brooklyn said in a scared, concerned tone. She dried her hands and then proceeded to sit on the bench against the wall. "I've had these numbing, sometimes sharp pains in my left side and stomach area off and on for the past few months. Sometimes, they're so sharp, I can barely talk or move."

"Could you be pregnant?" Shelbi asked, thinking Brooklyn could be experiencing signs of an ectopic pregnancy.

Brooklyn shook her head while rubbing her left side. "No. Wouldn't be possible."

"When was the date of your last cycle?"

"A few weeks ago."

"Is it always regular?"

"Yes, for the most part. Every twenty-eight to thirty days."

"Point to the location of the pain."

Brooklyn did so, and Shelbi felt her abdominal area, which was rather bloated and hard for a skinny girl.

"Are you on your cycle again?"

"No, but when I am, I have excruciating pains. I can barely walk. My thighs feel like bricks."

"Mmm. You could just be ovulating right now. A lot of women experience discomfort during ovulation with a light to sometimes hard pain in the ovaries. If it's been approximately two weeks since you started your menstrual cycle, ovulation may be the reason for today's pain."

"But I have pain during other times of the month as well." Brooklyn checked her watch. She took a deep breath, then stood. "My fifteen-minute break is almost up, and I can't have Rasheed looking for me."

Shelbi pondered over what could be causing the other pain.

"It could be fibroids, endometriosis, or cysts on the ovaries. Do you ever feel like something is pressing against your bladder during your cycle or right before your cycle?"

"Yes, and it hurts so bad."

Shelbi opened her wallet, pulled out a card, and handed it to Brooklyn. "My sister Raven is an ob-gyn. Call her and make an appointment. She's one of the best in her field."

"Thank you so much. I'll call her on Monday. Please don't tell Rasheed or Jay. They would worry, especially my brother."

"I promise not to tell anyone. Just make sure you go see Raven." Shelbi gave Brooklyn a big hug before she walked out of the ladies' room.

Shelbi stared in the mirror as she ran her fingers through her curls. She was glad to be able to help Brooklyn. She sighed, thinking about all that time she had spent in medical school. It wasn't totally wasted, she supposed. She knew a lot about the reproductive system and hormones considering that would've been her focus during her residency. She thought accepting the food critic position was the best plan, but now she wasn't so sure. She was still on an adrenaline rush from stitching up Justin's cut, and now she had given medical advice to Brooklyn.

I made the right decision. Right? I can't keep blaming myself for something that was out of my control.

Sighing, she shook her head. She was even more confused than before, but now wasn't the time to think about it.

When she returned to the table, Rasheed was sitting in her chair, talking to Bria. Shelbi smiled. They may be just friends for now, but she knew her sister. Bria had a weakness for handsome, suave bad boys, and eventually she would surrender to his game of seduction.

*****

Justin and Shelbi sat in lawn chairs in the afternoon sun at Tom Lee Park waiting for the results of the barbecue sauce competition. Justin and one of his line cooks had been cooking chicken, pulled beef brisket, and beef ribs since seven in the morning for the contest judges to eat with his barbecue sauce. Local restaurants, as well as those from neighboring states, were present, hoping to snag the first-place prize. All of the judges had tasted the sauces and were conversing in the judges' tent, deliberating on the results.

Shelbi read a fashion magazine while Justin sat quietly in the chair. His eyes were closed, yet he wasn't asleep. He had the earbuds of his iPod player in, bobbing his head to whatever the beat was. She knew he was nervous and listening to music was a way to calm his nerves.

Shelbi's cell phone rang. She glanced at the screen to see the name of the head food critic at *The Memphis Tribune* flashing on the screen.

"Hey, Sonya. What's up?" She bookmarked the article on how to please your man in bed, to give her colleague her undivided attention. She really wanted to know more about massaging the feet just right to hit certain turn-on zones on a man's body, preferably Justin's body. She had made up in her mind—she was going to seduce him tonight.

"I need a big favor, Shelbi. You know my trip to Vegas for the opening of Gary Joseph's new restaurant on the Strip?"

"Yes, you're leaving tonight on the red-eye. Right?"

"Wrong. I have a family emergency. My daughter has the chicken pox with a fever, and I can't leave her. Doug suggested you go in my place, but he needs an answer right away so he can have the travel agent change the hotel reservations and plane tickets into your name."

"Wow, I'm so sorry about your daughter. Um...sure, I can go." *There goes my plan to seduce Justin. Damn.*

"Perfect. I'll call him back now, and I'll e-mail you the information for the restaurant and what you need to be looking for. Shelbi, this is big. All the top food critics from newspapers and magazines from all over the country are going to the opening. This man has been cooking for over thirty years, so he knows what to expect and what the critics are looking for. Technically, it's just for fun, but still gather enough information for an article. E-mail me while you're there, and thank you so much. Expect Doug or the travel agent to e-mail you the itinerary. Your flight leaves at midnight."

"Midnight?" Shelbi repeated. It was three in the afternoon now. She would need to raid Bria's closet for shoes and

Raven's closet for clothes, then pack, wash her hair, and get a ride to the airport. *Maybe still seduce Justin? No. He doesn't want any time restraints.*

"Yes. Gotta go. Bye, and thank you again."

Shelbi sighed. She had already bought some sexy lingerie, gotten a Brazilian wax, and was trying to read valuable information on how to please her man in bed. She tapped Justin on the shoulder. He opened his eyes, took out his earbuds, and gave her a delicious smile, sending goose bumps over her body despite the eighty-degree temperature outside.

"Baby, I have news to share with you." She then proceeded to tell him her conversation with Sonya.

"So you're leaving tonight?" His face scrunched up into a frown.

"I'll be back this weekend."

"So, I guess I'm going to see Dr. Braxton by myself tomorrow."

"Baby, you'll be fine. There's nothing wrong with facing your phobia on your own. Sometimes, it's better that way. For example, I hate flying at night, but the flight leaves at midnight. Duty calls." She laughed nervously.

"I don't have a phobia of doctors."

"Oh, well, I certainly have a phobia of flying during the night. I keep thinking the pilots can't possibly see in the dark. It's not like there are streetlights thirty thousand feet in the air, but I'll be fine, and so will you. Hmm…can't wait to meet Gary Joseph!"

Justin nodded. "Gary Joseph is one of my idols. I love to watch him cook." He checked his watch and looked around the park. Shelbi knew he was anxious to hear the results. She squeezed his hand.

"He's amazing. I grew up watching his show, trying his recipes with my mom and grandmother. Now I get to meet him."

"A week without my Shelbi," he said, running a tender finger down her cheek. "What am I going to do?"

"I wish you could come. You really need a break. You work so hard, Jay." She cupped his face and gave him a tender kiss on his lips. He tasted like honey barbecue sauce.

Rasheed and Bria walked over and sat in their lawn chairs opposite Shelbi and Jay. They had just finished playing Frisbee with someone's dog and had come back to wait on the results. Bria grabbed a bottled water out of the ice chest and handed one to Rasheed, who gave Justin a hand dap.

"What's up?" Rasheed asked, throwing his long, muscular legs over Bria's. "Why y'all look so worried? My boy is going to win this, and then we're going to go party like it's nineteen ninety-nine. We should drive over to Tunica and stay at the Horseshoe Casino. I'll call this honey I know at the strip cl..." He took out his cell phone and then stopped and glanced at Shelbi, who was dying to hear the rest of his comment.

"Rasheed, don't stop because I'm here." She gave him a smirk.

Justin chuckled and squeezed Shelbi's hand. "Ignore Rasheed," he said to her and then looked at his homeboy. "He knows I don't go to strip clubs."

The announcer, a DJ from a local blues station, stepped onto the stage with the panel of five judges, who took their places at a table up front. Shelbi's heart stopped. This was it, Justin's big moment, and she was glad to share it with him.

"Can I have everyone's attention please?" the announcer asked as he stood on the stage holding four envelopes in his hand. "I have to admit, I tried all of the barbecue sauce entries. You're all winners in my book. I got a few bottles of most of your barbecue sauces in my pickup truck, but shh, don't tell the judges." The announcer laughed, as well as the audience and the judges.

"All right, folks, I won't keep you in the dark any longer. In my hand, I hold the four winners. One honorable mention along with the third, second, and of course, the grand prize winner."

A hush fell over the audience as the announcer opened the first envelope.

"All right, the honorable mention goes to Shack and Stack Barbecue from Clarksdale, Mississippi." The audience cheered as a team of three men walked up to the stage to accept their trophy and a check for $5,000.

Shelbi glanced at Justin, whose eyes were closed under his shades. She squeezed his hand a little tighter, and he kissed her hand tenderly and mouthed "thank you." When the third- and second-place prizes were announced, Shelbi felt his hand squeeze hers tighter, and his leg began to bounce up and down.

The announcer's voice became louder, and the audience grew quiet, waiting with anticipation. "This year's winner of the Pride of Tennessee's Barbecue Competition will receive a distribution contract with Pride of Tennessee Foods to make and distribute your winning barbecue sauces in the southeast region, including grocery stores in the states of Tennessee, Georgia, Mississippi, Florida, and Alabama. Y'all ready?"

"Yeah!" The audience screamed as loud as they could.

Rasheed stood and screamed, "Hurry up, man!"

Bria grabbed him and forced him back in his chair. "What I am going to do with you?" she asked.

Rasheed chuckled. "I can think of a few things…"

"Not in this lifetime, buddy."

Shelbi placed her attention back on the announcer, even though she made a mental note to speak with Bria one more time about Rasheed. He seemed like a fun guy, but she didn't want her sister hurt again.

Shelbi stared at Justin. "This is it, baby."

He smiled and closed his eyes again, still holding her hand.

"The winner of this year's grand prize goes to Chef Justin Richardson of Lillian's Dinner and Blues Club."

Shelbi screamed at the top of her lungs and kissed Justin all over his face. "Baby, baby! Get up! You won! You won!" She stood and pulled Justin up, who was apparently in shock.

"Man, you won!" Rasheed and Justin hugged. He also hugged Bria before taking Shelbi in his arms, picking her up, and twirling her around.

"What took you so long to get up, Jay?" she asked when he placed her back on her feet.

"I was still thanking God and my mother, baby," he said, and placed a tender kiss to her forehead.

Rasheed pushed Justin toward the stage as the crowd cheered and roared loudly, giving him a standing ovation. When he got to the stage, the announcer shook his hand and handed Justin a huge trophy. He kissed it and then raised it into the air.

The audience chanted, "Speech, speech."

He inhaled and exhaled for a moment.

"I'm truly humbled to be standing here. I've worked hard to get where I am, to own my own restaurant. Just like all of you did as well. I'd been working on different barbecue sauces, trying to perfect them, and then a cute, sassy little food critic told me my signature one sucked. Ha! The more I thought about it, the more realized she was right. I went back and changed it while still working on other ones. I need to thank the following people: My boys and business partners, Rasheed Vincent and Derek Martin, for having my back since I was four years old. Derek, unfortunately, isn't here. Someone has to run the restaurant. My girl, Shelbi, for telling me how she really felt about my barbecue sauce and helping me select the ones I entered in the competition. And last and never least, my mother for instilling in me the gift of cooking, humbleness, and bestowing on me unconditional love. I love you, and I miss you very much. I know you're smiling down on me because the sun is shining so brightly today. Also, thank you to the judges of the Pride of Tennessee for choosing my barbecue sauces as the winning sauces. Thank you!"

Justin stepped off the stage with his huge trophy and into Shelbi's waiting arms.

"Jay, I'm so proud and happy for you. I knew you would win."

"Thank you. I have a contract for my sauces, and I also have you. I'm the luckiest man on the planet."

CHAPTER TEN

Justin sat numbly in Dr. Braxton's waiting room the next morning. After dropping Shelbi off at the airport, he, Rasheed, Derek, and some more of their boys partied and celebrated until two in the morning. They didn't go to the strip club, much to Rasheed's dismay, but they still had a good time. Shelbi had called him at six to wake him up and to let him know she had made it to Las Vegas. She had slept most of the way on the airplane and was in good spirits despite her phobia of flying.

He wanted to tell Shelbi the real reason he had a disdain for doctors. It wasn't that he was some punk who was scared of seeing them—even though that's what she believed. He just didn't feel like talking about his reason yet. He already had enough of Reagan's lectures without adding Shelbi to the mix.

His cell phone beeped with a text message from Shelbi.

This hotel room is so nice. Lounging in this big, wonderful bed all by myself wishing you were here.

Damn! He was immediately aroused with passion for her. Her text only made him want her even more, but she was all the way in freaking Las Vegas. He texted back and hoped the receptionist wasn't paying him any attention. He figured the smile on his face had to be as wide as the Joker's.

Really? What would we be doing if I was there?

A reply came back quickly.

Whatever you want. Whatever you desire. I'm all yours.

He was about to respond, when he looked up to see Dr. Braxton enter the reception room. He was a young doctor, about his age, dressed in crisp tailored black pants, and a red polo showed under his opened white coat.

The doctor outstretched his hand with a polite smile. "Good morning, I'm Dr. Braxton, but please call me Garrett."

Justin hesitantly shook his hand and smiled at the doctor as much as he could. "Good morning, I'm Justin Richardson. Dr. Bria Arrington referred me to you."

Dr. Braxton nodded knowingly. "Yes, she contacted me the other day. Follow me to my examination room."

Justin trailed behind him. *So far, so good.* He wasn't nervous, but still somewhat uncomfortable, even though he sort of liked this man's personality.

They stepped into the examination room. Dr. Braxton washed his hands thoroughly, dried them, and then put on some gloves. "I'll just leave the door open. No other patients will be back here since we don't open until nine. You can sit up on the table and hold out the finger so I can take a look at it."

Justin held out his finger, and the doctor unwrapped the gauze Shelbi replaced last night before he dropped her off at the airport.

"Thanks for seeing me on such short notice and before hours. I appreciate it."

"No problem. When Bria said Justin Richardson needed his stitches removed, I couldn't say no. This looks healed." He nodded with an impressed smile.

"You know who I am?" Justin was surprised. He wasn't a celebrity chef, but Lillian's was the popular spot to hang on a Friday or Saturday night for blues and good food.

"I order food about once a week for lunch from your restaurant for my staff. We like the options of Memphis soul food and barbecue with a healthy twist."

"Wow, thanks for the compliment. I'm thinking about opening another restaurant in the near future."

"You should. I saw your interview on the news last night. Congrats on winning the barbecue competition. When can I start buying the sauces? I like the brown sugar one you introduced last week with the pulled beef sandwich. We ordered ten sandwiches with baked beans and coleslaw for lunch last Thursday."

"Really? Well, I tell you what, man, I'll bring you a couple of bottles this afternoon, on the house," Justin offered.

"Cool, and removing these stitches is on the house. You know, Bria did a good job." Dr. Braxton began to apply an antiseptic to the stitches.

Justin shook his head. "No, her sister Shelbi did it."

"Oh, Shelbi did this? Mmm…I'm impressed. It was my understanding she was a food critic now."

"You're right, she is. In fact, she helped me select the barbecue sauces to enter into the competition."

"Impressive. I don't know her personally, but she comes from a great family. I've known the Arringtons for years."

The Arringtons? I wonder if they're related to that son of a—

Justin's thoughts were interrupted when Dr. Braxton pulled the thread out through the skin. He winced and found a picture on the wall to concentrate on. It didn't hurt, but it was uncomfortable.

Dr. Braxton applied some antiseptic again. "You know, Justin, an idea just came to me. Have you heard of the Distinguished Men of Memphis?" He disposed of his gloves and washed his hands.

"They gave me a full-tuition scholarship to attend culinary school almost fourteen years ago. I donate every year to their scholarship fund to express my gratitude."

"Well, there's a scholarship fundraiser dinner coming up in a month. The restaurant that was going to cater the food pulled out this weekend for some reason. I'm in charge of finding another caterer quick, but companies seem to be booked already. Do you do outside catering? It's at the Cultural Arts Center."

"Man, I would love to do the fundraiser. I have a staff that does catering separately. However, since it's the Distinguished Men of Memphis, I'll come as well."

A look of relief washed over Dr. Braxton's face. "That's awesome. I knew there was something special about you."

"I appreciate that. When I stop back by this afternoon with the barbecue sauce, I'll bring the catering packet to you as well. My special events coordinator is Zaria Richardson. She'll create a fascinating menu for me to prepare. She also decorates the food tables beautifully with draped cloths, floral arrangements, as well as linens and centerpieces for the guest tables. Whatever you want, man."

"Sounds great. Is she your sister?"

"Baby cousin. She's very talented and creative. Whatever vision you have, Garrett, she'll take it and multiply it by a million."

"What a relief. I'm glad to have met you in person." Dr. Braxton extended his hand. Justin shook it and gave him a sincere smile.

Moments later, Justin was in his office e-mailing Zaria about the catering opportunity. She was off today, and he didn't want to call and disturb her. However, she was the type of person who checked her e-mail every other minute, and would receive it momentarily. He looked through the catering packet on his computer to print one for Dr. Braxton. He didn't want to look through Zaria's file cabinet while she was away since she was picky about people in her personal space.

A beep on his cell phone chimed. He received another text message from Shelbi.

Wish you were here. This bathtub is big enough for both us.

A rise in his briefs surfaced. He grabbed his appointment book. Brooklyn had written in the times for meetings and interviews for the next few days with the Pride of Tennessee representatives, up until Thursday at noon. Nothing for the rest of that day or the days following. He opened the Internet browser on his computer. He searched for the next twenty minutes, made a reservation, whipped out his credit card, and printed his receipt and the catering packet for Dr. Braxton.

A knock on his door sounded.

"Come in."

Rasheed entered looking tired yet spiffy in a brown suit and a plaid Burberry tie. He sat down in the leather chair in front of Justin's desk.

"Man, that was some night. After I dropped you off, Derek and I headed to the strip club. Boy, did we have fun."

"Why am I not surprised?" Justin commented. He handed the receipt he had just printed to Rasheed. "So, you ready to go to the Peabody for the meeting? Derek said he would meet us there." Justin stood, straightened his red tie, and put on his blue suit jacket.

"Umm...this is a receipt for a plane ticket to Vegas, leaving this Thursday at three in the afternoon."

"You may need to change the schedule for some of the line cooks this weekend. Call Carlos to see if he can work as well. Are we walking or taking the trolley?" He placed the packet for Dr. Braxton in his briefcase and grabbed a box with four bottles of the brown sugar barbecue sauce to drop off.

"You're going to Las Vegas?" Rasheed handed Justin the receipt and proceeded to the door.

"Yes, I am."

"To see Shelbi?"

"It's definitely not to see Chef Joseph."

"Man, you're whipped. That's my dog." Rasheed laughed as they walked down the hall to the front of the restaurant.

"Hey, man. Don't go telling your new friend, Bria, my business. I'm surprising Shelbi, and I'm not whipped." *Yet. I know I will be, though, once she gets through with me.*

A Cheshire cat grin formed on Justin's face, and he walked confidently with a little extra pep in his step and his friend laughing beside him.

CHAPTER ELEVEN

Shelbi stepped out of a long, refreshing shower in the oversized bathroom in her hotel room at the Bellagio casino. She had gone sightseeing and to lunch earlier in the day with her mentor and food critic, Tonya Clarke from Atlanta. She had taken Shelbi under her wing after they met at a restaurant Tonya was critiquing while Shelbi was a freshman at Spelman. Tonya had encouraged Shelbi to start her blog over seven years ago and had suggested she obtain her culinary degree since she had an interest in the food industry. She was forever grateful to Tonya and was glad to find a familiar face in Las Vegas.

Now Shelbi wanted to unwind and relax for the rest of the day. The food critics had been served breakfast at a cooking demonstration by Chef Joseph that morning. Tomorrow night was the grand opening of his restaurant, and then she would head back to Memphis on Saturday morning, where Justin would be waiting at the airport. She was looking forward to seeing him more than going to the grand opening.

There wasn't anything on the agenda for this evening. She could've gone to a show, but she wanted to look over notes and continue working on the article for the newspaper and its online blog.

She dried off and applied some baby oil to her legs, making them glisten like satin. *Too bad Justin isn't here to massage the rest of my body with oil.* She did her arms and stomach as well.

Shelbi was disappointed she hadn't been able to contact him earlier. He had called to inform her that his last meeting went well with the Pride of Tennessee representatives, and his lawyer hammered out a fair contract for him. She had called back to tell him she missed him, but his cell phone had gone straight to voice mail. She tried the restaurant, but Rasheed said Jay had stepped out. She wasn't worried, but she missed him and wanted to hear his deep baritone voice in her ear. She took off the shower cap and ran her fingers through her big curls, fluffing them out in a wild, sexy way.

She grabbed the hotel's complimentary bathrobe off the hook behind the bathroom door and proceeded out into the living area, onto the plush carpet. She grabbed her cell phone from the nightstand. No voice mail or text messages. *Oh well...*

She leafed through the Bellagio's room service dinner menu. Everything looked so appetizing, she couldn't decide. She wasn't really hungry, but she wanted something to snack on, even though she was still full from eating at Wolfgang Puck's Pizzeria and Cucina.

A knock at the door interrupted her perusing of the extensive menu. She ignored it. She had already placed the Do Not Disturb sign on the doorknob so the housekeeper wouldn't bother her.

The knock sounded again, and a man's voice with a French accent called out, "Room service."

Weird. I haven't ordered yet. Must have the wrong room.

She looked at the door to verify all of the locks were in the locked position and listened to see if the man had left. Her cell phone chime made her jump out of her skin. It was a text message from Justin.

Baby, are you out and about in Vegas?

She pushed the button to call him instead of sending a reply message.

She whispered into the phone, "No, in my room, but someone just knocked on the door, and I'm a little scared. Wish you were here."

He chuckled, and said in a low, sexy, tone, "Open the door, baby."

"But it could be a killer!" She tiptoed to the door.

"Shelbi, look through the peephole."

She peeped through and screamed for joy when she saw Justin on the other side.

"Oh, Jay!" She undid the locks and unbolted the door. She flung it open and jumped into his arms, placing kisses all over his face. "I can't believe you're here. I wanted you here with me so bad!"

"I know." He looked down at her, and that's when she realized her bathrobe was open. "I see you're ready for me."

"Yes, I am." She hadn't tied the belt, and now she was glad she hadn't.

He put her down inside of the room and retrieved his rolling suitcase from the hallway. He glanced at the Do Not Disturb sign and raised his eyebrow with a wicked smile. He closed and locked the door. His strong arms captured her, and his tongue buried into her mouth as if they were already one. She had never experienced so much pleasure from a man before, and it made her dizzy with passion. He tore off her bathrobe and pressed her up against the wall by the door, locking his lips with hers, creating an opus of joyous moans from her throat. She was thankful for the wall because she couldn't steady her legs or her breathing. When he let her go, she almost cried out no.

He stepped back as she stood panting, fighting for more air. A smile of admiration formed on his lips as he stepped out of his shoes and loosened his tie. His heat-filled eyes never strayed from her. They traveled over her body, which trembled in anticipation of what was to come. He shook his head back and forth with intensity on his face.

He whispered, "You're so damn beautiful."

Shelbi let out a ragged sigh, and tears welled up in her eyes. No man had ever told her that, and if one had, it wouldn't have mattered, because the words wouldn't have had the same effect on her. Justin was the only man her heart had ever longed and ached for.

*****

Justin had been waiting for this moment since he first laid eyes on the beautiful creature before him. Her naked, flawless body was quivering for him, and he intended to caress, pleasure, and love her until she was programmed to react only to his commands and touch.

He pulled her to him, and he felt her body tremble in his embrace. "I intend to drive you wild in every way I know how."

She sucked in her breath and gave him a sexy smile.

He had on too many clothes and began to unbutton his shirt. She finished the job, placing hot kisses down his chest in the process. He picked her up and carried her to the bed and laid her on the plush down comforter. Cupping her face, he kissed her softly on the lips before abandoning them to press kisses along her throat and collarbone, and then moved lower to grab a perky nipple in his mouth. After teasing it with gentle bites and sucks until it pointed at him, he then ravished her breasts with kisses, drawing subdued moans from her. Her fingers laced in his hair, her soft touches sending him into overdrive. He was ready to enter her, but he wanted to take his time, savor every inch of her smooth skin, and hear all of her erotic moans in his ear.

His tongue had a mind of its own, guiding itself down her stomach to taste the essence of her. She arched her hips as if she knew what he was about to do, whispering his name in a plea. He licked his tongue around the diamond stud in her belly button, then moved his finger down to her delicate softness and teased the bud of her womanhood.

He trailed kisses down her body and splayed his palms on her hips before dipping his tongue inside her entry, already dripping with sweet juices for him. She arched her hips and spread her legs to allow him more of her. He licked in and out of her, pleasuring the inside of her sugar walls, and grasped her rocking hips as she gripped the pillow, muttering his name. He swirled in sync with her hips, and when her pants turned into erotic gasps, he wasn't sure how much longer he could wait.

"What did you say, baby?" He lifted his eyes up so he could witness how his actions were affecting her. She was radiant. Her sweat had projected a glistening sheen over her body. Her passion-filled face held the look of readiness, and he was ready to give her all of him.

He replaced his tongue with his finger and inched his lips back up to her neck. She reached down and began trying to undo the buckle from his pants. He chuckled at her struggling.

"Please...Jay," she groaned.

"I'll get it, baby. Relax." He stood and in one swoop removed the belt and dropped his pants and boxers to expose his erect rod. She gulped, and her eyes widened at the size of his manhood. He strode over to his suitcase to retrieve a box of extra-large condoms.

He was so ready for her, he could hardly contain his emotions, but he wanted their first time together to be special and memorable. There was no need to rush. He lay down beside her, French-kissing her while he placed a finger inside her, stroking with a gentle glide.

"Please," she pleaded. "I'm ready."

He reached over on the nightstand to retrieve a condom. He kissed her forehead, her eyes, and nose before placing one hand in her hair. She rested her hands on his shoulders and took a deep breath.

He stared into her eyes as he slid his tip inside her, and then another inch at a time. She was so damn tight, he had to calm himself so he wouldn't climax. Her expression held a look of trust for him, and even when she sucked in her breath, her eyes never left his. He kissed her tenderly as he moved inside her at a slow pace. She whispered his name in between kisses, and a tear rolled down her face. He froze, thinking he had hurt her. He never wanted to cause his sweet Shelbi any pain. He almost pulled out, until a faint smile appeared on her lips and her hips moved up to his. She wiggled a little under him, exhaled, and wrapped her arms around his neck.

"I'm fine, Jay. You just feel so damn good."

With that reassurance, he began to move faster, stroking in and out of her until her wetness engulfed him. Breathless, angelic moans escaped her throat as his kisses matched his thrusts. Her tight muscles contracted and molded around his shaft, making his mind and heart sink further into her. When she began to match his thrust with her own, he lifted her legs higher around his torso and held her down by her hips. He pulled himself all the way out of her and then plunged back into her even deeper each time, sending her body into shudders, and louder screams of passion rose from her. She held on tightly to him, fingers digging into his shoulders, bound to leave marks, but he didn't care. Her passion was sending him over the edge, draining him of all coherent senses. He had never needed a woman like this before.

Shelbi began to move faster, pulling her hips and buttocks up to meet his rapid thrusts. He felt himself about to explode, and he lifted her legs over his shoulders to feel every single inch of her. He linked his fingers with hers and pinned her hands to the bed. When he roared out her name in the air and shivered hard inside her, she screamed his name in passion as she climaxed as well.

He buried his face in the crook of her neck, trying to control his heavy panting. He placed delicate kisses along her collarbone while she calmed her breathing with a smile. He hoped to be the only man to ever make love to her.

*****

Shelbi rested comfortably in Justin's strong arms, relaxing her head against his bare chest, listening to his heartbeat. If she didn't know any better, she could have sworn it was beating "Shel-bi." Silly, she knew, but with the way he called out her name, along with a plethora of curse words, at the height of his climax, what else could his heart possibly say?

They had just finished their second episode of lovemaking, and she was in a relaxed bliss. He was sleeping peacefully, snoring quietly every now and then. Justin made her emotions soar above the earth like an eagle with its wings spread, flying around carefree without a predator to touch her.

Their lovemaking had been intense, passionate—beyond what she thought was possible. He made her feel beautiful, desired, and sexy while fiery sensations raced through her veins. She sighed at the thought of making love to him again before the night was over and kissed him on the chest. He stirred, and she glanced up at his face. One of his eyes opened, and he stared down at her with a sleepy smile on his face.

"Girl, you wore me out." He sat all the way up against the headboard and pulled her into his arms. His stomach grumbled.

She laughed and rubbed his stomach. "Hungry?"

"Yes. I haven't eaten since the business lunch I had today. What time is it? Perhaps we can go down to one of the restaurants. There are plenty of them here."

"Cool. It's a little after eight. The Buffet is open until ten. I went the other day. Good food, but I need a shower first. Care to join me?"

An hour later, they were enjoying their buffet-style meal. They would've been down sooner, but being in the shower together had prompted another lovemaking session.

Justin laughed at the tower of food on her plate. "Baby, can you really eat all of that?"

"Probably not, but it all looked so good. I couldn't help it. I wanted everything."

"You're quite petite, besides those hips of yours. How do you manage to stay small and be a food critic?"

"I work out, and I usually don't finish meals when I go to restaurants to critique. For the most part, I just sample and take most of it home, especially if I visit more than one restaurant in a day. Besides, Bria prefers to finish my takeout for me."

"I'm so happy I came," Justin said, reaching over the table to hold her hand.

"I'm assuming you mean to Las Vegas and not the three times you came earlier," she answered in a sly tone.

"I just became aroused from thinking about it, especially in the shower with water running over you as I took you from behind."

Shelbi's pulse raced at the thought of them joined together in the shower less than forty-five minutes before. She had held on to the towel bar in the shower and placed one foot on the bench. Justin had pumped into her from behind, over and over again, until she'd had too many orgasms to count.

"Mmm…you were good. I'm glad we decided to wait until the perfect time."

"Me too." He took a swig of his bottled water and stared at her with a serious expression. "Shelbi, I'm planning a surprise birthday barbecue for my grandmother next weekend, and I would really like for you to go with me to meet her and the rest of my family."

"Jay, I would love to. How old will she be?"

"Eighty, but she swears she's only turning seventy, so humor her. She's very active. She still drives, but only during the day, and she's involved in different activities, like swimming and gardening. She's the reason why I have an herb garden at the center and at home. She planted them for me."

"I look forward to meeting her and the rest of your family. Are you doing all of the food for the party?"

"Of course."

"Well, I'll help you."

"Thank you. We can come up with a menu on the way back to Memphis." He sat back in his chair with a knowing smile. "We do cook well together, don't we?"

"We do. And now we have something else we do well together, too." Shelbi took her foot out of her shoe and rubbed her foot along Justin's pants leg. "In fact, I'm ready to make love again if you're game."

Justin tossed the napkin from his lap onto the table. "Check, please."

CHAPTER TWELVE

Shelbi and Raven sat outside of the Cheesecake Corner Café enjoying cheesecake and coffee a few evenings after Shelbi and Justin returned from Las Vegas. Shelbi was still in heaven over their time there, as well as their time together when they arrived back in Memphis. They had spent every night together and hated being apart from one another. She had planned to go to the restaurant tonight, but Raven wanted a slice of turtle cheesecake. Shelbi took notes and a few pictures of the café for her personal blog since she hadn't written any articles since returning from out of town.

She savored the tantalizing richness of her cookies-and-cream cheesecake. "Sis, I'm so glad you suggested we come here tonight. I haven't been here in a month, it seems. I live less than a block away, but I pretend it's not here. Otherwise I would have cheesecake every day."

"Girl, I know, and your hips do not need to spread anymore."

"Whatever. Justin likes them."

"I see he likes leaving marks on your neck as well. Make sure to wear a scarf or something when you go to his grandmother's house on Saturday."

Shelbi rubbed the spot where he had placed a huge hickey on her neck last night in the throes of passion. She giggled like a teenager.

"Thanks for the reminder. I doubt it will fade in two days."

"Nervous to meet his family?" Raven finished the last bite of her cheesecake, sat back, and patted her stomach with a satisfied grin.

"A little bit. We just started dating, so I was surprised he even asked."

"Mmm…interesting. Well, men just don't take anyone home to meet their family, especially the grandmother. I remember when I first met Howard's family, it was about two months into our relationship. It seemed he wanted his mother's approval. But you remember what a mama's boy he was. Luckily, she and I hit it off right away, and he asked me to marry him soon after."

Raven had a faraway, solemn look in her eyes, and Shelbi wished she hadn't started the conversation. She didn't want to remind her sister of the pain of losing her husband, even though Shelbi knew Raven still thought of him every second of the day. Raven fiddled with her wedding rings and wiped a tear from her eye with a napkin.

"How is his mother?"

"She's okay. I think she's stronger than me sometimes, always checking on me and bringing me food. I do the same for her, but it feels weird she's comforting me."

"Well, she loves you like a daughter. It's good you can be there for each other."

Raven nodded her head and finished her coffee. "Okay, another topic before I turn on the waterfall. What have you decided about starting your residency in January?"

Shelbi groaned in her head. Not this conversation again. She was still basking in the glow of her new favorite thing to do besides cooking—making love, and lots of it, with Justin.

"Honestly, I haven't thought any more about it. I've been busy with…" Shelbi paused. Busy with what? She hadn't critiqued any restaurants for the newspaper that week or worked on her blog. She'd been busy cooking up love with Justin.

"Busy with the handsome chef. Yes, I know. Well, I have a residency information packet for you in my tote bag. Don't shred it for Mr. Hamster either. Just think about it. You're a compassionate and caring person. The medical field needs more doctors like you who would place the needs of the patient first and go beyond the call of duty."

"Raven—"

"Wait, let me finish. I used to watch you when I first started working at the practice, when you worked in the reception area during your summers off. You were so concerned about the patients in the waiting room, seeing if they needed anything, bringing them water and holding their hand if they were in pain. Putting people's needs before yours has always been a part of you. For example, you're here with me right now because you know this is the first anniversary of my husband's death, and I sincerely appreciate it."

"Raven, I'm still working through my emotions right now. I feel as if I could've done more."

Raven opened her tote bag, handed Shelbi the packet, and looked at her cell phone as it chimed. "I understand, and I'm sure you did. But look at it this way, next time you'll do even more to help the patient. Every situation may not end in the results you or the patient's family hopes and prays for, but we don't make that decision. The man upstairs does. Don't worry. I won't bring this subject up again. I can't promise for the rest of the family, but I know you. You're a lot like Daddy. Both of you are determined, strong willed, and always make the best decisions."

"Thank you, Raven. I needed to hear that."

"You're welcome, and now I have to go to the hospital." Raven gathered her tote bag and purse. "I just received a text saying my patient has dilated seven centimeters. Thank you for keeping me company this evening. I appreciate it."

Shelbi gave her sister a tight hug before she walked across the street to her loft apartment. Once settled, she sat at her desk and read over the information Raven had given her and then glanced at the shredder. Sighing, she went to the closet and dragged out the box that held her medical degree and white coat. She put the coat on and dug out her stethoscope, which had been a gift from Cannon after she finished medical school. Placing it around her neck, she posed in the mirror. She smiled, remembering when she was a little girl and used to try on her mother's white coat and play doctor with her Barbie dolls and stuffed animals. The ringing of her cell phone snapped her out of reminiscing. Brooklyn's name displayed on screen.

"Hey, Brooklyn."

"Hey, Shelbi. I just wanted to tell you I saw your sister today, and you were correct. I have fibroids."

"I'm glad you found out the problem." Shelbi continued staring at herself in the mirror. "Are you going to have surgery?"

"Thinking about it. I also met with Bria briefly. She suggested alternative holistic methods, so I'm not sure. I'm just glad I know the reason for my pain, and both of your sisters recommended ways to help alleviate it."

"That's good. Are you going to tell Rasheed?"

"No, and please don't tell him. I can't have him worried about me. After our parents died, he became so overprotective, I can't breathe sometimes. I know he's a wonderful big brother, but he forgets I'm a grown woman. Once I'm done with my master's degree, I can stop working at the restaurant."

"I didn't know you were in school. What's your major?"

"Business, but I have to go now. My study group is waiting on me. I just wanted to tell you thank you for referring me to Raven. You were right on the money with the fibroid diagnosis."

"You're very welcome."

After hanging up, Shelbi admired herself in the mirror one more time. She ran a finger along her name printed in bold black stitch across the heart of the coat: *Dr. Shelbi F. Arrington, MD.*

Sighing, she took the coat off, folded it neatly, and placed it back in the box. She set the information packet on top, along with the stethoscope. She grabbed her overnight bag from the bed and headed out to meet Justin at Lillian's so they could ride the trolley together back to his home once the restaurant was closed.

*****

"They're going to love you, Shelbi."

"Really?" She sat in Justin's Navigator on the way to his grandparents' home for his grandmother's birthday party. The two of them had been up since five that morning preparing food at the restaurant for the barbecue. Shelbi's stomach was twisted in tight knots. She hadn't met anyone's family since high school. Justin's sister, as well as his aunt from Chicago, had flown in to surprise his grandmother, who helped raised him when his mother passed.

They pulled up into the driveway of an older brick home. Two men stood outside and walked toward the SUV.

"The one with the Memphis Grizzlies cap is my uncle Jeff, and the other one is my grandfather." Justin jumped out of the SUV and headed toward the trunk.

"Hey, nephew. We came to help. Sure does smell good," Uncle Jeff said before turning his eyes toward Shelbi.

"Uncle Jeff and Gramps, this is my girlfriend, Shelbi."

Shelbi shook their hands. "Very nice to meet both of you."

"Same here, little lady," his grandfather said. "Son, did you bring me some pulled pork and chitterlings?"

Justin handed his grandfather a pan. "No, Gramps. I brought pulled chicken, beef ribs, sweet potato salad, coleslaw, red beans and rice, turnip greens, and a Mississippi mud pie. No pork."

His grandfather laughed. "I'm just teasing, son. You know I don't touch that stuff anymore. Let's get inside with all of this food. Zaria stopped by earlier and set up the tables on the patio with beautiful bouquets of flowers. That girl sure can decorate. Reagan took your grandmother to get her hair done as planned. She just called and said they would be back in an hour."

"Perfect." Justin grabbed a pan and handed it to Shelbi and whispered, "See? You had nothing to worry about." He kissed her tenderly and then proceeded to the backyard.

Thirty minutes later, more family members and friends arrived for the surprise party. Shelbi met more uncles, aunts, and cousins. They were all pleasant toward her, and she felt right at home.

Justin motioned for everyone to be quiet. "Okay. Reagan just sent me a text. She's a block away. Let's go out to the lawn so Dear can see all of us when she pulls up."

Less than five minutes later, a sedan pulled into the driveway, with Reagan driving and his grandmother in the passenger seat with a surprised look on her face. Carrying a bouquet of roses, Justin's grandfather went to the passenger door and opened it.

"Happy birthday, my love." He handed her the roses and gave her a hug and kiss.

Everyone yelled out, "Surprise!" which was followed by hugs and kisses.

Justin and Shelbi waited on the porch. Dear walked toward Justin first, reached up, and pinched his cheeks.

"You did this, didn't you, son?"

"Yes." He turned toward Shelbi. "Dear, I want you to meet my girlfriend, Shelbi Arrington. Shelbi, this is my grandmother, Dear."

Shelbi held out her hand to shake hands, but his grandmother grabbed her with a hug.

"Nice to meet you, Mrs. Richardson. I've heard so much about you." Shelbi gave a sincere smile to the petite lady with the fresh silver curls touching her shoulder.

"Please call me Dear, honey child." She patted Shelbi's cheek. "It's very nice to finally meet you. Now, let's get this party started. You know I turned seventy today." She winked at Shelbi and walked inside holding Justin's hand.

*****

After everyone ate, Justin cleaned the kitchen while watching his family interact with Shelbi. He was glad his family liked her. She fit right in, joking with his uncle Jeff, discussing the latest shoes and purses with Reagan, and chitchatting with Dear about gardening. He smiled in their direction, and she patted Shelbi's cheek, which meant Dear really liked her. Upon noticing Justin, Dear stood up and walked toward the kitchen while Shelbi turned to talk to his grandfather.

"Need some help, son?" she asked, taking a dishcloth from the drawer.

"Uhh...no, Dear." He took the dishcloth from her. "This is your birthday party. Sit down and relax. You want some water?"

"Water? Boy, this is my birthday. Look in the cabinet above the refrigerator and pour your grandmother a shot—no, make it two shots—of Crown, with one piece of ice."

Justin chuckled and obeyed her. He joined her at the kitchen table with a bottle of beer.

"Did you have a nice time?"

"Yes. You really outdid yourself. I'm so proud of you and all of your accomplishments. And I especially like Shelbi."

"Really?"

"She's a keeper. She's a bold sister to put up with your perfectionist ways. I'm relieved she told you your barbecue sauce was a little too bland. Glad you stepped it up a notch before the competition. Just think, if she hadn't told you, you may never have changed it. You may not have won."

"You have a point, Dear."

"I know I do. Your grandmother may have just turned eighty, but I know what I'm talking about."

"Umm...don't you mean seventy?" he teased.

"All right, son. I can still put you over my knee." She laughed and took a sip of her Crown. "I like Shelbi Arrington. She's The One."

"Really?" he asked, even though he knew in his heart Shelbi was the woman he wanted to spend his life with.

"Your grandmother knows everything. Trust me, Justin."

*****

Later on that night, Justin held a nude Shelbi in his arms, thinking about what his grandmother had said about her being The One. They were relaxing in his bed after a long day with his family. His grandmother had always been right, and he trusted her judgment. She was the one who had persuaded him to apply for the scholarship to help pay for his tuition, had encouraged him to take a chance and open Lillian's, and even suggested he consider selling his barbecue sauce. She had been right about the other aspects in his life. Of course she would be right about Shelbi.

He kissed Shelbi on her forehead.

"You awake, beautiful?" He kissed her again.

"I am now." She laughed and climbed on top of his lap. Her nipples stared down at him. He reached his lips up and sucked one of them and then the other, her head cascading back with a sigh. Her lips sought out his, kissing him in a hungry and intense manner. He placed his hands in her hair, pulling her tongue deeper into his mouth, feasting on her delicious lips. They tasted like the piece of Mississippi mud pie she had just eaten before taking her shower.

She left his lips and placed kisses on his neck and ears. She trailed her tongue down his chest, swirling it around each nipple, then continued down his stomach. A feral moan escaped his throat as her tongue flicked inside his belly button and her hand ran up and down the length of his hardened shaft.

He placed his hands in her hair and held his breath at the possibility of her doing what he so badly wanted her to do. He lifted his head a tad to see her continue her tongue downward.

He felt the warmth of her mouth on the tip of his sex, licking the liquid that had escaped when he first realized her tongue was leading a trail there. She had never done this before, and he had never asked, but apparently she knew what to do, as she slowly took him into her mouth and let him slide back out again. The heat from her mouth was just as warm and wet as being inside her vagina, and he thrust his hips up to penetrate her mouth. A sweet moan emerged from her. She licked the length of his shaft, over and under it, while stroking it with her hands.

"Oh, baby, please don't stop!" he cried out.

When she placed all of his hardness as possible into her mouth and all the way out again, he shuddered as the majority of his length reached the back of her throat. He propped the pillows up on the headboard so he could watch properly.

"Damn...baby. Please do that again."

And she did, over and over, sucking him hard and long while stroking her hand up and down his slippery-with-saliva shaft. He didn't know how much longer he could stand it. He was going to explode any minute.

"Baby, come ride me."

She ran her tongue over his rigid shaft one more time and sat up with a lazy yet satisfied smirk on her face. He reached over on the nightstand and retrieved a condom. She took it from him and rolled it on before nestling all of him inside her. He could feel the tightness of her walls engulfing all him.

"Goodness, Justin!" she screamed out, riding him at a slow pace and then faster.

He guided her hips up and down with his hands, holding on to them tightly, and then reached behind her to spread her buttocks as he thrust up to meet her rapid movement. She rode him hard, her breasts bouncing in the air. Her orchestra of sounds was music to his ears as he continued to pleasure her.

Justin lifted her off him and placed her on all fours on the edge of the bed. He stood on the floor and took her from behind, causing her to scream out his name. He leaned over and kissed her neck and ears tenderly.

"What did you say?" he whispered and then kissed the back of her neck.

"Justin…" she moaned before letting out another scream of pleasure.

"Who's in control?"

She turned her head slightly to look at him with a sly smile. "I am."

He couldn't help but chuckle at her sarcastic remark. He thrust harder, pulling her butt to him.

"Who, baby?" he asked again, filling her all the way up with a long thrust. He stopped and sucked her neck where there was already a fading love bite.

"Mmm…um…mmm…uhh…ahh…mmm…you…" Her voice trailed off, and she slumped to the bed, flat on her stomach, bringing him along with her. Her muscles contracted around him as her orgasm escaped, causing her to shake under him.

"Justin, oh, Justin!"

She tried to bolt up, but he pinned her down to the bed, holding her hands to the mattress.

"Who's the only man ever to make you have an orgasm?"

"You, Big Daddy."

He continued to suck her neck and began to penetrate her again as she matched her rhythm with his.

Her hands dug into the sheets as he pumped in and out of her. He felt himself about to lose it. She started to move her butt back against him hard as his breathing became more rapid and his movements were no longer under his control. His orgasm was about to come hard and fast, and he held on to her tightly as if they were on a roller coaster. She was talking to him, coaxing him like a coach telling him to run the touchdown.

"That's right. Come, baby." She turned her head around to look at him. "Come hard inside me. Don't you forget who made you come this hard either."

"I...won't..." His body was buckling. He didn't know what was happening, but he no longer could control himself. He convulsed in a spasm against her. His muscles tightened, and then a rush of a hot, pulsating liquid spilled from him.

"Shelbi...damn...freak...got...Shel...ahh...shit..." He shook violently and then fell on top of her, breathing hard as hell. He kissed the back of her neck and then lifted his head and looked at her smiling, satisfied face.

"Humph," she started. "And you thought you were in control."

He laughed to himself. "I love you, Shelbi Arrington."

"I love you too, Justin Richardson."

CHAPTER THIRTEEN

Achoo. Justin sneezed in the middle of his lunch meeting with Anthony and Derek. "Sorry, fellas. I was saying, I'm...wait..." *Achoo*! He grabbed his napkin and stepped away from the table.

"Man, I got some cold and sinus medicine in my office," Derek said.

"Naw, I'm good. Just the change of seasons."

Derek shook his head. "You've been saying that since last night. Go home and get some rest. Anthony got this."

"Yeah, Jay. You need to go home. Besides, can't have you cooking and getting customers sick. Besides, it's Wednesday. We won't be that crowded tonight, anyway. Rest up for the weekend." Anthony patted Justin on the back.

Justin sneezed again and nodded his head in agreement. The rumbling of the mucus made his chest hurt every time he sneezed. They were right. He needed to rest.

"All right, I'm outta here."

He left the upstairs dining room and waved and nodded to the lunch customers in the main dining area while he headed to his office to grab some things and make a phone call.

"Hello?" Shelbi's sexy voice answered in his ear.

"Hey, baby. I'm going to have to cancel our movie date tonight...Wait..." *Achoo.* "I'm..."

"Sick," Shelbi finished for him. "I told you that this morning when you left for work. Have you taken anything besides the vitamin C?"

"Not yet. Derek has something in his office—"*Achoo.* "I'm on my way home."

"Okay. Once I finish this article, I'll come over with all the medicine you need."

"Mmm...baby, I can't wait. I may have to be on the bottom. I'm a little weak at the moment."

"I meant real medicine. I'll see you in an hour."

"Thanks, babe."

*****

An hour later, Shelbi was in Justin's kitchen juicing oranges as she waited for the water to boil for his echinacea tea. Bria had suggested some cold herbs, and Shelbi had stopped by the health food store to get them. The aroma of celery and rosemary filled her nose from the homemade chicken noodle soup. She hoped it would loosen his mucus. He'd been sneezing, but his nose was stuffed up, and he couldn't blow. Luckily, he didn't have a sore throat, but she had brought some lemon and honey as well.

She made a tray with the soup, juice, and tea and carried it to his bedroom, where he rested.

"Hey, Big Daddy." She set the tray on the nightstand and sat on the edge of the bed, placing her hand to the back of his neck to see if he was warm. He was propped up on pillows and watching the sports channel.

"The soup smells good, sweetie." He turned to her. His eyes were weak, and his nose had turned red from all of the blowing, even though nothing had come out.

"I'm going to take your temperature. You don't look or feel feverish, but it's best to know." She reached into her tote bag and grabbed an ear thermometer and a stethoscope.

"I see you came prepared," he said, picking up the stethoscope.

"I just want to check the congestion in your lungs. Sit up."

"Is that all Bria's stuff?" he asked, eyeballing her medical instruments.

"Yep. I have a bagful of her old medical instruments she used during her residency."

Shelbi placed the stethoscope around her neck and then turned on the ear thermometer.

Justin jumped when he saw the thermometer and scooted away from her. "Where is that going?"

"In your ear, silly. Where did you think it was going?"

"Just checking. Looks like one of those kinky toys you women have."

"Ha ha. I don't need those. I have a real man with a nice package to satisfy me. Now be quiet."

She checked his temperature. "It's ninety-eight point nine. A little elevated, but I can get it down to normal. Now, sit all the way up and take off your shirt," she said, placing the stethoscope in her ears.

"What are you doing?"

"You said it felt like mucus was in your chest. Now hush, and take a deep breath for me."

Shelbi placed the stethoscope on his chest, then on his back, and listened as he breathed in and out.

"Mmm…I can definitely hear the mucus rumbling, but your heart sounds perfect. It's beating my name. Go ahead and put your shirt back on, and drink the tea and soup. They'll help loosen the mucus so you can either blow or cough it up. I'm going to call Bria."

"Thank you, baby. You've been wonderful." He took a sip of the tea and continued watching *Sports Fanatic*.

She went back to the kitchen to straighten up and to call Bria, who was at work.

"Arrington Family Specialists, this is Lana. How can I help you today?" Lana had been the office manager since the practice opened.

"Hey, Ms. Lana. It's Shelbi. Is Bria available?"

"Well, hello, Dr. Shelbi. Dr. Bria is right here. I'm going to transfer you to her office. You know, we're all praying that you change your mind. We could use your bubbly personality around here."

"Thank you, Ms. Lana."

Moments later, Bria answered her phone.

"This is Dr. Bria Arrington," she answered in a professional tone.

"Girl, you know it's me."

"Whatever. How's your patient?"

"He's fine. Just a little congested. I gave him some echinacea tea, vitamin C, and some of my homemade chicken noodle soup. But that's not why I'm calling. I think I'm ready to tell him I'm a doctor."

"Really? It's about time. What made you come to that decision?"

"Well, lately, I've considered starting my residency, and I'm ready to tell him what I've been going through. I've come to terms with what happened during my internship. Now, I'll know better for the next time."

Bria sighed with relief. "Baby sis, I'm so proud of you. Can't wait to tell Daddy!"

"No! Don't tell him yet. I haven't made a final decision, but I'm ready to tell Justin about my experience. I love him. I want him to know everything about me."

"I'm so happy for you. Can at least I tell Raven?"

"Yes, but no one else, not even Mommy. Okay? Gotta go check on my man!"

Shelbi went back to the bedroom to find Justin resting peacefully. His soup and teacups were empty, as well as the glass of orange juice She took the dishes away, cleaned the kitchen, and then went back into the bedroom to watch over

Justin. She had brought her laptop and did some work on her blog while he rested.

While she worked, she found herself glancing at the man she loved. He was so handsome, caring, and confident. She knew whatever decision she made about starting the residency program, or continuing with her job as a food critic, he would be supportive. She was still reluctant, but taking care of him this afternoon had made her realize maybe she could give it another try.

"Hey, beautiful," she heard a groggy voice say.

She smiled and looked up at Justin, who sat up against the headboard. She went over and propped the pillows up behind him and grabbed the thermometer from the nightstand to check his temperature again.

"Good. It's normal. How do you feel?"

"Better, especially since I woke up from my nap and found my beautiful nurse staring at me. Thank you for taking care of me, Nurse Arrington."

She laughed and took a position at the other end of the bed. She wanted to cuddle with him, but she didn't want to get sick too. She had taken some vitamin C and drank a cup of echinacea tea earlier to prevent catching his cold.

"Hmm…I prefer Dr. Arrington over Nurse Arrington," she said, thinking this would be the best time to just go ahead and tell him. She took a deep breath.

"Hmm…I like Nurse Arrington. You would look hot in a cute little nurse outfit with some red heels. But either way, you've taken such good care of me. Thank you. Your bedside manner is perfect. You can be my nurse anytime." He gave a laugh that ended in a cough.

She stood and pulled the cover up to his chest before sitting next to him.

"You know, women can be doctors as well, Justin."

"Baby, I'm not calling you a nurse because I'm against women being doctors. I just don't care for doctors at all, minus Bria, and I like Dr. Braxton. He's cool."

"I thought you conquered your fear of doctors when you saw Dr. Braxton."

"Baby, I don't have a fear of them. I don't like doctors because they don't care about saving lives. They only care about all the money they make off of a patient. A patient dies, and they move on."

"Justin, that's not true at all. Doctors go through a lot more than you realize. It hurts to lose a patient, knowing you couldn't do anything to save them no matter how hard you tried."

"Shelbi, don't take it personal. I like Bria. She and Dr. Braxton seem like two of the rare ones who care."

"Justin, where is all this coming from? I never realized you felt this way. I assumed you just had a fear of doctors."

"Baby, did I tell you how my mother died?"

"You told me she died from complications during open-heart surgery."

"True, but the surgeon could've done more to save her. Instead, he rushed out of the hospital so fast in a tuxedo—like he was late to a party."

Damn. Now what? Do I still tell him about my dilemma?

"Justin, doctors take their jobs very seriously, but things happen that are out of human control. Unfortunately, situations don't turn out like we always want to. You were only twelve. You don't know what the surgeon did or didn't do."

"Shelbi, I hear you, and I know your sister is a doctor, but you weren't there. I don't hate all doctors, I guess. Just the asshole of a surgeon who didn't save my mother. He could've done more, baby."

Shelbi nodded her head. He could be right. There were some doctors who truly just didn't care. She had met some during her internship who were cold and gave up easily if they felt nothing else could be done. She was glad she came from a family of doctors who cared about the well-being of their patients. Especially her father, who believed in the importance of saving lives and never rested until all options had been exhausted.

"And you're probably right." *Okay, here it goes.* "Jay, I need to tell you—"

"No matter how long I live, I will always hate Dr. Francis Arrington, the surgeon who let my mother die on the operating table."

CHAPTER FOURTEEN

Shelbi thought surely she was in a nightmare. She looked around the bedroom. There weren't any monsters coming from the closet, and the boogeyman wasn't about to grab her leg and pull her under the bed, even though she sort of wish he would. Instead, the television was on mute, the sun had gone down, her computer screen had a slide show of puppies going across it, and her body was hot, fever hot, with numbing tingles shooting through her. She had to have misheard what Justin said. Surely, he didn't just say her father, her hero, her daddy, her first knight in shining armor, was the surgeon who let Justin's beautiful mother die when he was only twelve.

She looked up to see Justin's mouth moving, but no sound came out. Her body was sitting there, but she had been whisked away to an episode of *The Twilight Zone*. The man she loved would hate her in a minute if she opened her mouth. Her breathing became irregular, her mouth dry, and the ringing in her ears was so damn loud she wanted to scream. But she didn't.

"I'm sorry, baby. I think...I'm coming down with your cold. I feel a little hot." She went to the window and opened it to let the cool autumn air touch her face. "Did you say something else? I tuned out for a moment."

"I said, are you related to Dr. Francis Arrington? I thought about it at Dr. Braxton's office. That would be so crazy, right, if you were related to him. But I was just joking. Come lie down in the bed. We can be sick together."

She laughed nervously as she ran her hand through her hair. "Oh, no. Um..." She closed the window and grabbed her tote bag.

"You're leaving?" He sat all the way up and swung his legs over the edge of the bed.

"Yeah, I need to go before I catch your cold. Just continue taking the herbs Bria suggested every four hours, along with the fresh-squeezed orange juice with some ice. It's in the fridge."

"Yes, Dr. Arrington." He stood and pulled her to him, kissing her lightly on the forehead. "You know, babe, you would make a better doctor than a nurse. You gave the type of care I wish my mother would've had. Thank you for taking care of me. I wish you would stay, but I don't want you sick. I love you, Shelbi."

Tears welled in her eyes, but she shut them off. She would have plenty of time to shed them later because she knew she could never see him again. Cold be damned, she kissed him hard, pulling his tongue and mouth aggressively to her. She inhaled his intoxicating masculine scent she remembered getting a whiff of when they first met. She ran her hands over his hard, comforting chest as she stared into his eyes, which held so much love for her she almost shook herself awake from the nightmare she was in. She kissed him with all the passion she could, telling him with her eyes, tongue, and hands she loved him and always would.

*****

Shelbi had called Bria and Raven on three-way and explained everything that had happened. They had agreed to come over after work to comfort her. In the meantime, she had to make a very important phone call.

"Hello, Shelbi, dear. Glad to hear from you," her father said.

Shelbi took a deep breath and a sip of her white zinfandel.

"Daddy, do you remember a patient named Lillian Richardson? She died about twenty years ago."

Her father remained silent, and she assumed he was thinking. He'd been a cardiologist and surgeon for over thirty years. She didn't know why she expected him to remember her, but she just needed to know.

"Yes. She was one of my favorite patients. Great family. Her mother is still my patient. Feisty old lady. Just turned eighty not that long ago. Why, Shelbi?"

"Umm...well, I'm sort of dating her son."

"Jeff? He's a little too old for you, and married, young lady."

"No, Daddy, *Lillian's* son. Justin. Do you remember him?"

Her father let out a long sigh. "Small world. Yes, I remember the little boy who hated me, and still does, I believe. He was so angry at me the day his mother died. He cried and begged me to try one more time to save her. I felt so bad. She was the first patient I had ever lost. I went to the funeral, and he accused me of killing his mother. But I understood. I had lost my mother when I was only a teenager. He's grown into a fine young man, with a very popular restaurant. I had no idea you were dating him."

"He's a wonderful man."

"I know he is. I've kept up with him over the years through his grandmother. I tried reaching out to him when he was in high school, but he didn't want to be bothered with me. When I saw his name on a scholarship application for the Distinguished Men of Memphis college fund, I immediately wrote a check for his full tuition to the culinary school."

"What! Oh my goodness. You paid his tuition! Does he know you paid for that?"

"No, baby girl, I wished to remain anonymous. Besides, it was through the organization. He now donates every year to the scholarship fund."

"Oh, Daddy, I don't know what to do."

"Well, what did he say when you told him you're a doctor and I'm your father?"

"He doesn't know any of that. I was going to tell him, but...never got around to it. And I need to tell you about something that happened during my internship."

Tired of keeping her emotions and guilt bottled inside, Shelbi decided to let everything out. She went on to explain to her father about the patient and Dr. Clouse, as well as her conversation with Justin earlier.

"Shelbi, I already knew about the incident during your internship. I just wanted you to work through this yourself in order to grow and become the doctor you're meant to be. However, if you aren't ready, I won't pressure you anymore. I know it had to be devastating. Trust me, I've been a doctor for many years, and it still hurts my heart when a patient dies, especially after I've done everything I can to save them. You'll know the moment when you're ready. Your mother went through something similar, which was why she was a stay-at-home mother for years."

"Thank you, Daddy, for understanding. Wait, who told you about the incident during my internship?" Shelbi asked, thinking Raven and Bria couldn't keep their mouths closed.

"You forget, I know everyone at the medical center in Nashville where you did your internship. When are you going to tell Justin?"

"I'm not. I broke up with him. He just doesn't know it yet."

"Oh, I see. Well, that's a decision you'll have to make on your own. I'm sure Bria and Raven will give their two cents."

"Of course. They're coming over now."

"Shelbi, I'm sorry you have to go through this. I'm sorry what happened over twenty years ago is causing you unhappiness, but remember, what doesn't kill you will make you stronger. I love you, Shelbi."

"Love you, Daddy.

*****

Justin sat through a meeting with the executives from the Pride of Tennessee Foods. He wasn't really listening. He didn't even need to be in the meeting, but he figured it would get his brain off of Shelbi. His mind stayed on her channel no matter how hard he pushed the button on the remote. His thoughts wandered back to the last conversation he had with her five days before at his home. It had replayed so many times in his head, it had scratches and pauses. *What did I say to make her not want to see me anymore?* He had called, texted, even gone by her apartment, but her personal code to enter the building had been changed. As he had entered the meeting, she responded in a cop-out text, finally, after five days of unreturned phone calls and text messages.

You haven't done anything wrong. It's me. I just need to move on. Please understand.

Please understand what? That they were so perfect together? They loved to cook, play pool, listen to the blues, stare at each other and not say a word, cuddle, make love. What was the problem? She had met his family, his friends and had a key to his place. He'd never done that with any other woman.

After the meeting, he called Rasheed, hoping he knew something, anything, that maybe Bria had said since she'd become his new best friend.

"Look, for the last time, Bria won't tell me anything. All I know is Shelbi wants to move on, but it's not you, it's her. However, I just spoke to Bria, and both sisters are across the street from their apartment building, at Arcade Restaurant for lunch, but you didn't hear it from me."

"Thanks, man."

Thirty minutes later he spotted the sisters leaving Arcade just as he descended from the trolley. She looked beautiful, yet tired. Red eyes, slicked-backed hair, no makeup, and a jogging suit. It appeared their breakup was rough on her as well. However, she had dumped him, and now he needed answers. He stepped back behind the corner of the building so she couldn't spot him and run the other way. The sisters were chatting as they approached, and he listened with curious ears to what Bria was saying.

"If you'd just been honest with him, you may still be together."

"It's not that easy, Bria."

He stepped out from behind the corner and grabbed Shelbi to him.

"What's not that easy, Shelbi?"

"Justin!"

"I need to know! What's the problem? Why have you been avoiding me for almost a week and then send me an 'it's not you, it's me' text message this morning? What's going on?" He looked down at Shelbi and then to Bria for some answers.

Shelbi stepped back from him and held on to Bria. "Don't you tell him anything!"

Justin breathed out a groan and spoke to Bria as calmly as possible. "Bria, what's going on? You just said she needed to be honest with me. You *were* talking about me, right? What is Shelbi hiding?"

"Justin, my loyalty lies with my sister, but..."

Shelbi stepped away from her sister and stood in front of him. She placed a hand to his cheek and the other one over her heart.

"Justin, right now, I have a lot on my plate with things I can't even begin to tell you about." A tear ran down her cheek, and he wiped it away as another one came in its place. "I don't need to be in a relationship right now. Please try to understand. It's complicated and..."

"Baby, whatever it is, we can deal with it."

She shook her head and walked toward the glass door entrance with Bria, who mouthed the words "I'm so sorry" to him.

"I love you."

Shelbi stopped in her tracks at his words. She had her hand on the handle of the door as Bria typed her code into the keypad. He could see Shelbi's reflection through the glass panel. Tears ran down her face. Her mouth was open as if she were about to speak, but instead she opened the door and closed it without looking back.

CHAPTER FIFTEEN

"Zaria, the banquet hall looks exquisite. You did a great job, cuz."

Justin gazed around the Cultural Art Center's banquet hall where the Distinguished Men of Memphis scholarship fundraiser banquet would soon begin. He and Carlos had just finished setting up the Sternos for the chafing dishes, and Zaria was putting the finishing touches on the centerpieces.

"Thank you. I hope Dr. Braxton likes it. He's such a picky man. I almost threw my portfolio at him during our first meeting." She placed the last calla lily in the vase in the center of the buffet table and stood back to admire the scene.

"Well, I'm glad you didn't. But I like the white roses tied with the brown-and-blue ribbon on the guests' tables. Very chic."

"Thanks. Here he comes now." Zaria rolled her eyes and tossed her hair over her shoulder.

As he approached wearing a tuxedo with a brown-and-blue bow tie, Justin could've sworn Dr. Braxton gave Zaria a once-over and then bit his bottom lip. She was quite beautiful with her long hair cascading in curls down to her waist, and a gold strapless dress that stopped just above the knee, which complemented her toffee-colored skin.

"Do you approve, Dr. Braxton?" she asked, looking around the ballroom.

"Very, very beautiful, indeed, Ms. Richardson," he said and then turned to Justin. "The food smells delicious. I can't wait to eat, man."

"Thank you. If you two would excuse me, I need to go finish up," Justin said.

The banquet began an hour later. Justin decided to stay in the kitchen and let Carlos and the chef over catering take care of refilling the chafing dishes. There was a carving station and a stir-fry station that were being handled by two of the line cooks. Speakers were in the kitchen of the facility, so he was able to hear the presentations on the stage. He could've gone out and watched, but he wanted to be alone with his thoughts.

He was still in a foul mood. It had been a week since he'd last seen Shelbi. He hadn't called her, even though he had considered it. He tried to stay busy and focus on future plans of opening another restaurant, possibly in Germantown or Midtown. Derek had been putting together a business plan as well as overseeing the barbecue sauce project. Justin had plenty on his plate without having to concern himself with what the heck Shelbi wasn't being honest about. He missed her like crazy, but if she couldn't tell him, then maybe she wasn't the woman for him.

He tuned in his ears to what Dr. Braxton was saying.

"It is with great pleasure that I bring to the stage the man who has graciously been the founder and committee chair of the scholarship fund for twenty years. He has helped raise thousands of dollars to send young men to college who may not have had the chance because of financial reasons. Because of his vision and passion for education, we've had many success stories with the young men we've helped achieve their goals. I'm proud to say I was one of the recipients years ago. It is because of the Distinguished Men of Memphis and his vision that I'm a doctor. Ladies and gentlemen, please help me applaud Dr. Francis Arrington and his family for their wonderful contributions to our organization. Dr. Arrington, will you and your family please come to the stage?"

"What?" Justin dropped the knife onto the counter and rushed out to look at the man he hadn't seen in twenty years. He stood in the back, next to the buffet table. There he was, Dr. Arrington, on the stage, shaking hands with Dr. Braxton. He had aged some, of course, his head covered with salt-and-pepper hair. He was slightly bigger, but not overweight, and now wore glasses. Dr. Arrington turned around and motioned for his family to come up. An older, attractive woman sashayed over and kissed Dr. Braxton on the cheek, followed by two men in tuxedos and three sexy young women. He looked harder at the women. *Could it be?* But there on the stage, hugging Dr. Braxton, were Bria and Shelbi. She had on a short, formfitting red dress and those damn red pumps. The dress was hitting her hourglass figure in all of the right places, accentuating her sexy curves. A rise in his briefs jumped up, but now wasn't the time.

What the hell was she doing up there? She said she didn't even know Dr. Francis Arrington when he had asked her on the day...damn, on the day he told her about his mother's death, which was the same day she abruptly left his home and his life. Now he knew what Bria was telling Shelbi she needed to be honest about. Was she a cousin? He'd learned through the grapevine that all of Dr. Arrington's children were doctors at his practice. *But wait, Bria and Shelbi are sisters, and Bria more than likely works there...*

Justin's mind was boggled with all kinds of scenarios as to how Shelbi was related to Dr. Francis Arrington.

He gave his attention back to the stage as Dr. Arrington went to the podium.

"Thank you so much for the warm applause. I feel humbled and blessed to be a part of such a wonderful group of distinguished men. But tonight isn't about us. It's about raising money to send young men with dreams and ambitions to college. I used to be one of those young men years ago. I grew up in Hurt Village. We were so poor, I wore the same outfit to school sometimes two or three days in a row and not because it was a school uniform. When my mother died, I was sixteen. That was a very low point in my life. I had no idea how I was going to pay for college, but I knew I had to go. I knew I had to get myself and my two younger siblings out of that situation and help others when I was able to. I made a promise, which is why I created the scholarship fund to help other young men. My wife and I are very blessed, and we would like to present a check for fifty thousand dollars tonight."

The audience cheered and clapped, as well as his family onstage, all of whom were smiling, except Shelbi. She had a solemn look in her eyes, and Bria glanced at her and smiled, which made Shelbi give her a fake smile. Shelbi's eyes roamed the audience, and then they settled on him. She jumped, and placed her hand over her heart. She nudged Bria and whispered something to her. Bria looked in his direction, her eyes widened, and she nodded to acknowledge him. He nodded back.

"My wife and I are very proud of our children. They have decided to match what we're donating, and they're each giving ten thousand apiece. My children are all doctors in our family's practice. Cannon, Raven, Sean, and Bria currently work there, and my youngest daughter, Shelbi, just graduated from medical school in May and will hopefully begin her residency soon."

Justin stared straight at her. He couldn't believe everything he had heard. The woman he loved was the daughter of the surgeon who let his mother die, and to top it off, she was a doctor as well? Well, that explained a lot. She could stitch up a cut, use a stethoscope, had messy handwriting, and had a great bedside manner, in more ways than one.

Why didn't she tell me she was a doctor, though? Why keep it a secret?

Now he knew why Shelbi was jumpy the night she sewed up his cut and had rushed Bria out of the loft. She had called her "Dr. Shelbi," but he hadn't realized Bria meant it literally.

He stared back at her hard. She stared back, not blinking, with a scared look on her face, and her breasts were rising up and down a little too fast, causing him to want to kiss them despite the fact he was angry. His emotions were running haywire. He loved her, but she was the daughter of the man he despised the most in the world.

*****

Shelbi stood numbly on the stage as her father continued his speech. She could feel the anger in Justin's eyes penetrate through her like a tiger ready to jump his prey. Her heart was beating loudly against her chest, and her hands were clammy. He now knew everything. Not only was she a doctor, but her father was the man Justin had hated all these years. When her father finished, Justin turned to head back to the kitchen with a scowl on his face. She immediately left the stage and dashed after him, her stomach in knots and her head spinning from the champagne, but she had to get to him.

She found him alone, his back to the kitchen door, hands clenched on the prep counter. Her heels clicked on the tiled floor. He breathed out a long sigh and held his head back and then down again, but he didn't turn around.

"Jay…"

"Not now."

"When?"

He turned to face her with so much coldness in his eyes she almost didn't recognize him.

"When, you ask? You had plenty of moments to tell me."

"Can we step out back? There's a gazebo where Raven got married."

He closed his eyes and breathed deeply. "Okay." He motioned for her to walk in front of him.

They went out the door and followed the trail to the gazebo. It was chilly out, and Shelbi had forgotten her wrap at the table. She wrapped her arms around herself and sat on the bench under the gazebo. He unbuttoned his chef coat to reveal a long-sleeved shirt. He handed her his coat.

"Thank you." She put it on, inhaling his wonderful scent and feeling the warmth of his body radiating from the coat. She had missed his scent and his presence so much, she pressed the coat closer to her, trying to block out the tears.

"Why didn't you tell me you were a doctor? That's not something to hide. It's an accomplishment. Something to be proud of."

"It isn't when..." She took a deep breath. "During my internship earlier this year, a patient under my care died." She proceeded to tell him the story.

He was silent for a while, but she didn't say anything. She sat anxiously waiting for his response.

"Are you going to go back?"

"I don't know. That was so hard. I don't want to go through that again. My parents and my siblings are wonderful doctors. What if I don't measure up? What if it happens again?"

"Why didn't you tell me all of this sooner?"

"Justin, I didn't want anyone to know. My own family had no idea what had happened until recently. They all thought I was being rebellious because I'm the youngest. I just wanted to move on, and when the opportunity came for me to be a food critic, I accepted the position. I wanted to bury my medical career. I didn't tell you because I was ashamed. I could've done more, and I didn't."

He stooped down in front of her and wiped the tears from her face. He was so close, she wanted to reach out and kiss him, beg him to forgive her.

"You could've told me."

"I was going to, but then you said my father was the man that didn't save your mother, and I froze. I knew how hurt you've been because of your mother's death. I didn't want to add to it, and I thought it was best to..."

145

He stood up and stepped back from her as if she had just reminded him about the white elephant in the room. He turned and faced the building, his back to her.

"My father lost his mother when he was a teenager. The doctors at the clinic weren't giving my grandmother the proper care. He decided he would become a doctor so people in that position would be given the best care despite their income bracket or whether or not they had insurance."

"Humph." He turned to rest cold eyes on her. "I guess my mother wasn't part of his plan."

Anger boiled in her, and she stood to face him, but she calmed down her nerves so she could speak to him without making the situation worse.

"Justin, my father is a wonderful, wonderful man who cares about you and your family a great deal. He remembers that day, and I remember, too. I was six years old. He came home late. He'd gone to a dinner party with my mother. I was waiting up for them with my grandmother. We'd baked cookies, chocolate macadamia nut, just for him. He picked me up, hugged me, and said, 'I had a bad day, Shelbi, love. I lost one of my favorite patients.' Then my mother said, 'Time for bed.' I pretended to go upstairs, but instead, I hid in the dining room. I heard my father crying. I'd never seen my father cry, which is why I always remembered that day. The next day, he asked me and my grandmother to bake a few more dozen of the chocolate macadamia nut cookies because he said the little boy of the lady that had died liked them. That was you, baby."

"I ate every last one of them in my bed after the funeral," he said in a whisper to himself, yet she still heard. "I didn't realize where they had come from."

"Justin, I'm sorry I didn't tell you sooner that I'm a doctor."

"You should complete your residency."

"It's not that easy. What if…"

"So, you're just going to quit? After my mother died, did your father quit? He didn't. Last I heard, he's a very successful, renowned cardiologist."

"I'm not my father. I'm scared to fail again."

"What were you going to specialize in?"

"Internist, focusing on endocrinology, but I don't know if I am now."

"Wow. So you're giving up just like you gave up on our relationship?"

"What was I supposed to say when you told me that my father is the surgeon you've hated all this time?"

His voice rose with anger. "The truth! I asked you if you were related, and you said no and then ran out of my home and my life."

She stood in front of him, searching his face, trying to find some trace in his eyes that he still loved her.

"Would it have made a difference? Would you have still wanted to be with me? I love you with all my heart, Justin, but I'd understand if…" She stopped. She couldn't get those words out.

He was silent for a moment. He closed his eyes and placed his hands on top of his head and then ran them down his face. When he spoke again, he spoke softly—the anger in his voice had vanished.

"I don't know, baby." He paused, running a finger down her face, making tears run out of her eyes. "I don't know if I can be with the daughter of the man I despise. I'm sorry, Shelbi. I hope everything works out and you make the right decision about your residency. Even though I don't care for doctors, you would be a good one. You're caring and compassionate, and after the experience you had during your internship, it will only make you a better doctor. I know it's not your fault who your father is, but I need time to process this, and right now isn't the time. I need to get back to work."

With his hands at her waist, he pulled her close and tenderly kissed her on the lips. He cupped her face, drawing solemn moans from her throat.

"Now I know why the kiss that day felt as if you were telling me good-bye." He kissed her forehead and headed toward the kitchen door, leaving her outside.

A few moments later, after crying her eyes out, she stopped in the ladies' room to wash her face and then went back into the kitchen. Justin was preparing the coffee and cappuccino on a cart. She took the jacket off and handed it to him without speaking. He handed her a cappuccino, and she took it, avoiding his eyes. If she looked at him again, she knew she would cry.

"This should warm you up," he said.

"Thank you." She hurried out of the kitchen before she broke down again.

She managed to make it back to her family's table. Luckily, the only one there was Bria, sending text messages. Her parents mingled with the guests, and Sean and Cannon were dancing, being the life of the party as usual, stepping and throwing up their fraternity sign. Poor Raven looked bored to death with some old geezer in her face.

She wrapped her shawl around her shoulders and took a sip of her cappuccino, which was made exactly how he knew she liked it. She almost turned on the water faucets again, but didn't. Instead, she turned toward Bria, who was busy giggling like a teenager with her first crush.

"Who's that?"

Bria looked as if she hadn't realized Shelbi had rejoined her. "Nobody," she said, tossing the phone into her purse.

"Well? What did he say? Is he really mad at you?"

"Um…yeah. He doesn't want to see me anymore, which I already figured would happen. Now it just makes it harder."

"Shelbi, I'm sorry. I had no idea Lillian's was catering until we saw him. Rasheed said he was holding down the fort because Jay had a catering gig. What are you going to do?"

"Move on. Focus on my career, my life."

"Which career?"

"I don't know. Right now, nothing even matters because Justin isn't a part of my life anymore."

CHAPTER SIXTEEN

A loud ringing made Shelbi throw back the covers and hit her alarm clock, but the noise didn't stop. She spotted her cell phone on the dresser and stumbled out of the bed toward it. Not recognizing the number, she didn't want to answer it, but she did anyway since it had awoken her from her not-so-peaceful slumber. It had been a week since the banquet, and she'd had restless nights ever since.

"Hello?"

"Ms. Arrington?"

"Yes?"

"Hi. This is Myra from the community center. How are you doing today?"

"Hello, Myra, I'm doing well." She had met the receptionist when she assisted Justin with his cooking class.

"I wanted to tell you that all of the picture consent forms have been returned from the parents, so you can conduct your interview and take pictures for your blog."

"Oh, that's good." *No, it's not! I forgot, and now I can't possibly go with Justin there.*

"Are you able to come this Monday? I'm looking at the menu Chef Richardson e-mailed me. He's teaching the students how to make shrimp bisque with a chickpea-and-lentil salad. He could probably use your help since Carlos won't be able to assist him."

"Um...sure. Hold on, let me check my planner." She grabbed it out of her laptop bag next to the bed. She barely knew what day of the week it was. The days had run together, but she was almost certain it was Saturday. "Sure, Myra. Please let Chef Richardson know I'll be present."

"Okay, dear. See you Monday. Make sure to stop by the office to get a volunteer badge and sign the volunteer sheet."

"No problem."

On Monday, Shelbi walked confidently toward the kitchen classroom an hour before the class was to begin. Myra had called earlier that morning to inform her Chef Richardson wouldn't be able to attend the class because of a meeting, and could she teach the class since it was her recipe he was using? He had already bought the ingredients and dropped them off earlier with a lesson plan on his desk.

Per his instructions, she set up the stations accordingly and placed the students into three groups of three. When they arrived, they were glad to see her. The students put on their chef jackets and read over their copies of the recipe.

"Excuse me, Ms. Arrington, but where's your chef jacket?" Bobby asked.

"Oh...I forgot it. But I'll be fine," she answered, looking down at her cream sweaterdress and camel boots. *Great, of all the days to forget my jacket and wear cream.*

The young lady she remembered from the last time, who did an excellent job with the sweet potato pie, approached her. "You can wear Chef Richardson's coat. It's long enough to cover your dress. He leaves it hanging behind the door of his office," Hannah said as she went to retrieve it.

"Thank you." Shelbi took the oversized jacket and put it on. A hint of his cologne was still on it, and she had to catch herself from crying. She missed his scent so much, she had bought a small bottle of the cologne he wore just to smell him again. But it hadn't helped because it still didn't smell like him.

An hour and a half later, the groups' bisques were done, along with the salads and a Memphis mud pie. She took pictures of the students while they prepared their dishes, and also offered advice as they cooked. Hannah had really impressed her with her careful making of the pie, even though she had snapped at the two boys in the group when they didn't want to use accurate measuring for the vanilla extract.

"Hannah, I'm very impressed with your dessert skills." Shelbi sat down at a table with the teenager who was still fuming over her group not wanting to make it per the recipe.

"Thank you. Chef Richardson says I should think about becoming a pastry chef. While I do like cooking entrées and side dishes, desserts are my favorite. I love watching cake decorating shows on the Food Network. I can see myself doing that one day." Hannah's attention was diverted over Shelbi's head, toward the door.

"Chef Richardson!" they all screamed as if a celebrity had just entered the room.

Shelbi's heart stopped, and heat rose in her face. *Why is he here? I thought he wasn't coming because of some supposed meeting.*

She turned her head in his direction. He was surrounded by the students giving him hugs and hand daps, but his attention was on her. Her lips parted as his eyes roamed over her before settling on the name on her jacket. He raised an eyebrow, and a small grin swept his face.

He was mouthwatering in a dark blue suit, a blue shirt, and a paisley tie with a matching handkerchief in the pocket. She was glued to the chair, her hands semi-clenching the table.

"Okay, my future master chefs, let me see what you guys did with Chef Arrington." He followed behind the groups to their individual areas.

He stopped at Bobby's group. "Wow. This tastes as good as Chef Arrington's bisque," he said, turning his eyes on her as all of the students did as well.

Shelbi simply nodded and smiled at the students, afraid to say anything for fear it could come out like a croak. She could've sworn sex and lust were in Justin's smoldering gaze, and she needed to escape fast.

Justin instructed the students to go ahead and eat their meals and then clean up because it was almost time for them to depart. Shelbi walked around and snapped a few more pictures as a distraction away from Justin. He joined a group of boys, even though she could feel his strong gaze on her. She felt naked and vulnerable.

"Why you late, Chef, and all suited up? Did you have a court date, man?" Bobby asked.

Justin broke out in a loud laugh, the one she loved to hear. It was good to hear his laugh, and Shelbi had to place her focus on wiping down the counters to keep her attention off him. But it was hard. His commanding presence lit up the room, and she sensed him watching her, despite his conversation with the boys.

"No, son. I had a very important business meeting today."

Since she noted his serious tone, and he was "all suited up," as Bobby had mentioned, she had to admit maybe he really did have a meeting and wasn't trying to avoid seeing her.

"But you never schedule things during our class. You always come no matter what. Rain, sleet, snow, you're always here," Bobby said.

"I know, and trust me, I hated not being here. I always try to stay committed to my obligations, but I knew you were in good hands with Chef Arrington. She can cook almost as well as me, and since she's wearing my coat, I'm sure everything turned out well." He gave Shelbi a wink, which caused her heart to flip-flop.

"We didn't want her cream sweaterdress to get any stains on it. It's a hot dress!" Hannah said, snapping her fingers in the air.

Justin raised his eyebrows and smiled wickedly at Shelbi. When he stopped smiling, she noticed a slight gulp of his Adam's apple. "Oh really? Well, that's very nice of you guys to look out for Chef Rich...Arrington."

After the students finished cleaning their stations and left, Shelbi went to the back office to take off Justin's coat and gather her belongings.

"Hey there." He poked his head into the office, startling her. He walked in, his suit jacket in his hand, thrown over his shoulder. He took a seat on the desk and loosened his tie. Her heart thumped so loud, she was sure he could hear it. His tight, muscular thighs showed through his pants, and the tightness of his abdomen, which she knew oh so well, rippled through the shirt. The office was barely bigger than a broom closet, and being close to him in the small space made her want to help him finish taking off his tie, shirt, and pants.

"They're a good group of future chefs. I enjoyed working with them." She closed the door slightly to hang the coat back on the hook.

"I appreciate you taking over for me today. I found out about the meeting this morning and asked Myra to give you a call."

"I was surprised she called. You could've called yourself."

"I didn't know if you wanted to hear from me. But I really do appreciate it."

"You're welcome. I enjoyed teaching them. Now, I need to jet." She glanced at her watch.

"Cooking dinner for Bria?"

"No. I have to go to Germantown tonight." She reached across him to grab her purse and jacket off his desk, her breasts brushing his arm.

"Damn! Hannah was correct. That dress is hot! Shows all those hips just right. Where are you going? Hot date?" he asked sarcastically.

"I don't know about hot, but Raven and Cannon have set me up on a blind date with a frat brother of his."

"Who the hell are you going out with?"

"Pardon me? We aren't together anymore. I can do as I please. Now if you would excuse me, I need to go."

He grabbed her by the waist, pulling her body between his hard legs. He kissed her hungrily as erotic moans escaped both of their throats. Their tongues intertwined in a fast groove. She had missed him so much she had almost forgotten where they were. She pulled back from him.

"We can't do this," she said, trying to catch her breath, which he'd taken away with his hot kisses. "What if someone walks in?"

He jumped off the desk, closed the door, and locked it before he grabbed her and pushed her against the wall. He showered kisses down her throat and lifted her dress, sliding one of his hands into her panties. One finger slid into her wet center, followed by another one.

"Oh, Justin," she whispered, her hands clinging to his hair as he continued sucking and kissing her neck.

He unbuckled his belt and unzipped his pants, then yanked them and his boxers down to the top of his shoes. He pulled her panties down, and she flung them over one of her boots. He lifted her by the buttocks as she wrapped her legs around his waist and held on to his shoulders.

He whispered into her ear, kissing it at the same time. "I bet the jerk you're going out with tonight will never make you feel like this, will he?"

"No."

He thrust into her over and over, finding secret hidden spots inside her she didn't even know existed. She called out his name in a whisper, begging him to go faster and deeper as he stroked her. Tears burned her eyes, and her fingernails clenched his shoulders as he continued the rhythm of going in and out of her. His hands dug tightly into her buttocks as he walked with her to the desk and laid her down on it. He bunched up his jacket as a pillow for her head. He leaned over and kissed her on the lips and pulled her legs over his shoulder.

"Baby, you feel so damn good." He sunk further into her, releasing an untamed groan from his throat. He held her hands hard to the desk, pumping in and out of her, sending quivers throughout her body. She had missed his kisses, his lovemaking, and the way he said her name

She needed to feel all of his hardness inside of her, and she thrust up her hips to meet his feral rhythm.

His name started in her chest, but it couldn't get past her throat as her moaning and irregular breathing took over. She no longer cared they were in his office at the community center. She had needed and desired him for weeks. His breathing, thrusts, and groans were becoming faster as he plunged all the way into her, spilling his seed inside her. He crashed on top of her, burrowing his head in her shoulder. He lifted his head to look at her moments later, after their breathing had returned to normal.

"Justin, what are we doing?"

"I don't know. I missed you. I saw you. I wanted you, and you wanted me. It was all over your face when I came into the classroom."

"You clearly don't want to be with me, yet we just made love." She turned her eyes away from his face thinking about the mistake they had just made.

He rose slowly, stood, and backed himself against the wall as he pulled on his clothes.

"Baby, I didn't say I didn't want to be with you. I just can't come to grips with who your father is."

She got off the desk and looked around for her panties. She spotted them on the other side of the chair and put them back on. She pulled down her dress and gathered her purse and coat.

"Justin, I love you, but I'm not going to sit around and wait for you to decide. I know losing your mother hurts, and I know you thinking my father is at fault is a hard thing to deal with. But I know my father. I'm sure he did everything in his power to save your mother."

He remained quiet, his eyes in a distant place. She kissed him on his cheek and reached for the door.

He spoke in a quiet tone. "I have some things I need to work out. But I love you. Don't think for one minute that I don't."

"I know." She opened the door and bolted quickly out of the office and the classroom. She held the tears in as she walked to her car. She called Raven and told her what happened and that she wouldn't be able to meet Cannon's fraternity brother for dinner. She just wanted to go home and have one last cry alone.

*****

"Why so quiet, Justin?"

Justin looked over at his grandmother sitting in the passenger seat of his Navigator. He was taking her to her weekly bingo night at the community center. His thoughts were on Shelbi, their lovemaking from thirty minutes ago, her father, and his mother. He was still in shock that out of all the women in the world, he had fallen in love with the daughter of the man he hated.

"Nothing, Dear. You have everything you need?" he asked before he backed out of the driveway.

"Yep. Ready to play bingo. Are you going to stay and play basketball with some of the kids?"

"Yep. Rasheed is doing a basketball clinic, and I told him I would come by and help."

"So, what's eating at you, and don't say nothing again because I know when you lie. It's about Shelbi and her father?"

"Hmm...Dear...I don't want to talk about it. It's over. We have officially ended our relationship."

"You hate him that much to give up the one woman you've ever loved?"

"She was my mother, and he didn't save her!" He raised his voice and then regretted it as soon as he did. He glanced at his grandmother, praying she wouldn't slap him into next week.

"She was my daughter, and he did do everything possible, despite the fact your mother signed a Do Not Resuscitate form before the surgery."

Justin almost ran into the back of a car. He regained his composure and focused on the road.

"What do you mean she signed a Do Not Resuscitate form? Why would she do that?"

"She was tired, baby," she said softly. She reached out to hold Justin's hand. "She was very ill. She made me and Dr. Arrington promise that if anything happened, we would make sure you and Reagan were taken of."

"But..." Justin didn't know what to say. Why would his mother want to die? If she was ill, he would've taken care of her, worked three jobs. It didn't matter. She was his mother, and he loved her.

"Dr. Arrington, despite the form, tried saving your mother. He's a good doctor and a good man. He didn't want your mother to die either, but people know when it's time, and your mother was ready. She just wanted to be at peace. I miss my daughter every day, but I'm glad she doesn't have to suffer anymore."

Justin remained silent. Tears welled in his eyes. He had to stay strong and focused so he could get his grandmother safely to the community center. There were so many thoughts swirling around in his head as he tried to process this newfound information.

"Dear, I had no idea. Why didn't you tell me years ago, when it happened?"

"You were a child, and when you got older and moved on, there wasn't anything to say."

"Did you know who she was when I brought her to your birthday party?"

"Yes, Dr. Arrington is still my doctor, and he talks about his children all the time. There are family portraits in the waiting room at his practice. Justin, the Arringtons are a family of caring doctors. Dr. Arrington kept his promise to your mother. Remember the scholarship you received from the Distinguished Men of Memphis? He funded that out of his own pocket and paid for your entire education."

Justin pulled into the parking lot and parked his SUV at the front of the building so his grandmother wouldn't have far to walk.

He shook his head in disbelief.

"I had no idea. Why didn't you tell me?"

"I thought if you knew the money came from him, you wouldn't accept it. He called me to make sure you had applied for the scholarship through the organization. He said he would donate the amount you needed and make sure you got it."

He squeezed his grandmother's frail hand before kissing it. "I'm sorry I raised my voice earlier."

She laughed. "I know, son. You've been angry for a while. I just want you to be happy. I know Shelbi is the one for you."

"Why do you say that?"

"Baby, when you were about five or six, me, your mom, and you went to Dr. Arrington's office for your mother's checkup. We waited in the waiting room. His wife, who was six months pregnant at the time, came to take her husband to lunch. She and I started talking about names for the baby. She mentioned about five different names she liked, including Shelbi. You looked up from your comic book and said you liked that one out of all of the names she had suggested."

"Wait? Are you telling me I suggested her mother name her Shelbi?"

"Yes, which is why I know you two are meant to be. Now, I need to go inside so I can win some money for this cruise I want to take this summer." She leaned over and kissed him on the forehead. He got out of the SUV and walked around to open the door and help her down.

"Thank you, son. See you in a few hours."

Justin parked the SUV, turned off the ignition, and rested his head back on the headrest. He closed his eyes and let out a long sigh. He tried to process everything his grandmother had told him. His mother had signed a form that she didn't want to be resuscitated if anything went wrong during the surgery. His emotions were mixed. Even though Dr. Arrington tried to save her anyway, he was still torn. He'd been a child when it happened. All he knew was that Dr. Arrington had made him a promise before the surgery. He had trusted the man, looked up to him. He'd thought he was invincible and could do anything, like a superhero. But he was just a man, and at the end of the day, only the man upstairs had the final decision on death.

CHAPTER SEVENTEEN

Shelbi looked over the photos she took of the cooking class the previous day. She'd gotten the images printed from her digital camera at the drugstore and was waiting for the trolley. She needed to go to Beale Street to interview a chef for an article, and she figured she would drop the pictures off at Lillian's because she had promised the students she would make sure they saw them. Her goal was to leave the pictures with the hostess to give to Justin. It was lunchtime, so hopefully he would be in the kitchen.

Upon walking into the restaurant, she saw Justin speaking to a customer. She hoped he hadn't noticed her, but his eyes met hers instantly. Her breath caught in her throat, and her shoes stuck to the floor. He gave her a wide smile and came forward.

"Hey, Shelbi."

"Hey. I just wanted to give these pictures to you from the class last night." She held out the envelope containing the pictures.

"Thank you. Um...do you have a minute? I need to talk to you. I called you several times this morning, but your phone kept going to voice mail."

She nodded. The phone wasn't off, but whenever she saw his number, she purposely sent the call to voice mail, but he never left a message.

"I really don't have long. I have an interview in a few minutes."

"Can we step back to my office?"

"I can't stay long."

A woman's scream from the upstairs dining room sent Justin and Shelbi bolting up the stairs.

"Is there a doctor in the house?" a man called over the banister.

"Yes!" Shelbi called out.

When they got to the second floor, a lady was trying to give a man the Heimlich maneuver, but his face was turning blue.

"Lay him on the floor quickly!" Shelbi said. "Justin, call nine-one-one."

"All right, people, step back and give Dr. Arrington some room!" Rasheed commanded.

As a couple of the male customers helped lay the man on the floor, Shelbi spied a wrapped straw in a waiter's apron and a steak knife on the table. She opened the straw and cut it in half with the knife.

"Are you his wife?" Shelbi asked, undoing the man's tie and shirt quickly.

"Yes. Please save my husband. The food is lodged in his throat."

"Just hold his hand. Sir, this may hurt a bit, but you'll be fine in a minute."

With the steak knife, she made a half-inch-deep horizontal incision between the Adam's apple and the cricoid cartilage. Then she pinched the incision and inserted the straw one inch deep. She blew two quick breaths into the straw, paused for a few seconds, and then gave one breath every five seconds until his chest rose and fell. Shelbi let out a sigh of relief, and the customers cheered.

Moments later, the paramedics were placing the man on a gurney.

"Miss, you did a fine job saving his life," one of the paramedics said.

The man's wife walked over and gave Shelbi a warm hug. "Thank you, thank you for saving my husband's life. I love him so much. I wouldn't know what to do without him. What hospital do you work at?"

"I'm not at a hospital. I just completed medical school."

The paramedic nodded. "Well, you did a fine job saving his life. You'll make an excellent doctor."

A few minutes later, Shelbi sat on Justin's couch thinking about what had happened. She had called the chef she was supposed to interview and explained she wouldn't be able to make it. They rescheduled for the next day.

Justin walked into his office with a glass of white zinfandel and a tray of food.

She laughed. "You should've brought the bottle," she said, reaching for the glass.

"Shelbi, I'm amazed at what you just did. You saved that man's life. You were so serious. You immediately took over the situation and handled it calmly. I would've panicked."

"Can't panic in moments like that. You have to stay focused, or the person could die, and I couldn't let him die," she said, wiping a tear away. He joined her on the couch and pulled her onto his lap. She rested her head on his chest and closed her eyes, breathing in his scent.

"You smell like barbecue sauce."

"You think I should make it into a cologne?"

She giggled. "Um...no. Justin, I'm ready to complete my residency. I'm not scared anymore," she whispered.

He kissed her forehead. "I'm glad to hear. You'll be a wonderful doctor, Dr. Shelbi F. Arrington. What's your middle name?"

"You don't want to know."

He kissed her softly on the mouth.

"Frances. My father wanted my first name to be Frances, but my mother said no."

"Shelbi, I need to tell you something, which is why I've been calling you all morning." He proceeded to tell her everything his grandmother had relayed to him last night.

"So, you helped my mother pick my name?" she asked, a little bewildered. She got up and went to the table where he had placed a plate of barbecue beef brisket sandwiches, catfish, and sweet potato fries.

"Apparently, I don't really remember."

"Wow."

"But it just proves one thing."

"What's that?" she asked, dipping a piece of catfish into the tartar sauce. Since their breakup, she had barely eaten, but now she was famished.

"We were meant to be together. Can we try again?" he asked.

"What about your feelings for my father?"

"I did a lot of thinking last night, and after witnessing you save that man's life, I now know in my heart that doctors can save lives and that your father tried his best. I was just a child when my mother died. I've had this grudge ever since against him. Now it's time for me to move on, hopefully with you."

He walked over to the table, grabbed her from her chair, and held her close to him. She looked up at him, running her finger along his name on his jacket.

"Justin, I think it's time you meet my family."

*****

Shelbi gazed out the window of Justin's SUV as they drove to her family's weekly Friday night dinner. She was ready to announce to her family she would continue her residency and was glad that Justin would be by her side. She had stopped by Memphis Central Hospital earlier in the day and turned in her information packet.

Bria sat in the backseat texting and giggling, more than likely with Rasheed.

"Justin, it's the third house on the left." Shelbi pointed and then took the remote for the gate out of her purse.

"House? You mean mansion, don't you?" he asked as they pulled up to the two-story brick home with the four-car garage, and tall white columns on the front porch. The home sat at least half a mile away from the street.

"It is a big house, but now that it's just my parents, they're considering downsizing. I think they like South Bluffs."

He parked behind Raven's Mercedes, and they got out as the front door to the home opened. Bria grabbed the pans in the backseat and handed one to Shelbi. Shelbi's mother, Darla, stepped out wearing a blue pants suit belted at the waist. She was still petite despite having five children.

"Hello, my beautiful daughters. And who is this fine young man?"

"Mom, this is Justin Richardson."

"Nice to meet you, Dr. Arrington." He gave her a hug.

"Please, call me Dr. Darla. If you say Dr. Arrington, seven heads will turn in your direction." She laughed and looped her arm through his as they walked toward the house.

"No problem, Dr. Darla."

"Well, it's about time I finally get to meet you again. You know, you helped me decide my baby girl's name. Let's go inside. Everyone is waiting. What's in the pans, girls?"

"I made pad Thai and breading pudding," Justin answered.

"Mmm...I see someone told you Dr. Francis's favorite dessert and that I like Thai food." She turned and winked at Shelbi.

As they entered the house, Shelbi looked nervously for her dad. "Where's everyone, Mother?"

"In the family room, dear."

As they entered, Shelbi made the introductions of her brothers and Raven. She noticed her father wasn't in the room.

"Where's Daddy?"

"He's in the study," her mother said as her father entered the room, his eyes going straight to Justin's. The room grew silent, and all eyes were on the two men. They stared at each other for what seemed like hours, and Shelbi's heart beat rapidly against her chest, waiting for one of them to speak. She knew Justin had been nervous with mixed emotions of finally facing her father.

"Good evening, Justin. It's good to see you, son." Dr. Arrington walked over and shook Justin's hand.

"It's good to see you as well, sir."

"Let's step into my study. Darla, go ahead and let the kids eat. We'll be back."

During dinner, Shelbi could barely eat her food as she wondered what on earth her father and Justin were talking about. Thirty minutes had gone by, and they still hadn't emerged from the study. Her mother smiled at her reassuringly as her brothers discussed their next golf trip and whether or not they thought Justin would like to come. When she saw her mother's eyes look up and a smile spread across her face, she turned to see Justin and her father walk into the dining room laughing and talking as if they were old chums.

Justin sat down next to Shelbi and began to spoon some of the pad Thai onto his plate. She gave him an "is everything okay" stare.

He leaned over and kissed her forehead and whispered, "Everything is fine."

After dinner, they all relaxed in the family room, eating dessert and drinking coffee or wine. Shelbi decided now was the time to make her announcement to her family.

She tapped her fork on her wineglass. "I have an important announcement to make."

"Wait," Justin said, standing. "Before you make your announcement, I have one as well."

He kneeled in front of her. She sucked in her breath as goose bumps formed a cold wave on her. Her breathing became faster, and she tried to calm herself, but she couldn't help it. Bria rubbed her back to calm her nerves. She closed her eyes and opened them to see a three-karat princess-cut diamond ring in a black velvet box in Justin's hands. Her hand flew to her chest, and oohs and aahs sounded from her sisters and mother.

"Oh, Justin, baby…"

"Shelbi Frances Arrington, will you marry me?"

"Yes! Yes!"

He took her trembling hand from over her heart and placed the ring on her ring finger. They kissed tenderly, forgetting they weren't alone, until Sean suggested they get a room.

"When do you want to get married?" Justin asked as her sisters and mother admired the ring.

"Well, soon, because…" She took a deep breath as she got ready to share her big news.

"Because what, sweetie?" her mother asked.

"After careful consideration and contemplation, I've decided to begin my residency in January at Memphis Central. I turned in my information form today and gave *The Memphis Tribune* a month's notice. I have orientation in the middle of January."

Her family cheered and hugged her.

"Well, we have two things to celebrate tonight—no, wait, three," her father said. "My daughter has finally decided to complete her residency, I've gained a son-in-law, but most importantly, it's Justin Richardson. You were like a third son to me when you were growing up, and now I'm happy to officially say, welcome to the family." He shook Justin's hand and gave him a hug.

After dessert, Shelbi and Justin relaxed on her parents' veranda to have some alone time together. She sat in his lap and sipped on champagne while she admired the huge rock on her finger.

"Justin, what did you and my dad discuss for so long? I thought you two would never come out."

"I told him I was sorry for avoiding him all these years, and he said he understood. I thanked him for the scholarship, and he asked me to assist him with the committee."

"So, you're going to join the organization?"

"Yep, next month. I also told him I loved you with all my heart and wanted to marry you."

"Justin, we should get married before I begin my residency. I won't have time to plan a wedding once I begin."

"Perfect. The sooner, the better. How about Christmas Eve?"

"That's a good idea. I love you, Chef Richardson."

"I love you too, Dr. Arrington."

The End

ABOUT THE AUTHOR

Candace Shaw is the author of fun, flirty and sexy African-American contemporary romance novels. She is a PRO member of Romance Writers of America and Georgia Romance Writers. She is also a member of Alpha Kappa Alpha Sorority, Inc.

When Candace is not writing or researching information for a book, she's reading, window shopping, gardening, listening to music or spending time with her loving husband and their loyal, over-protective weimaraner. She is currently working on the next novel in the Arrington Family Series.

Feel free to drop her line at Candace.Shaw@aol.com or visit her website at http://CandaceShaw.net

*****

Books by Candace Shaw

Arrington Family Series

Cooking Up Love
The Game of Seduction (Available as an ebook in September 2012 & print in Winter 2012)
Only One for Me (Available as an ebook in Winter 2013 & print in Spring 2013)

Chase Family and Friends Series

Perfect Candidate for Love (Available as an ebook in Spring 2013 & print in Summer 2013)

THE GAME OF SEDUCTION

Please enjoy an unedited preview of the next book in the Arrington Family Series, **The Game of Seduction**. The ebook version will be released in September 2012 on Amazon, Barnes & Noble and All Romance eBooks. The print version will be released in Winter 2012. Subscribe to

http://www.CandaceShaw.net for updates.

Chapter One

"Take one Clarinex every morning until you completely run out, even if everything clears up," Dr. Bria Arrington instructed her patient who had broken out in hives after eating shellfish. Bria scribbled out the prescription and handed it to the young woman.

"Thank you. Next time, I'll make sure to ask what's in the gumbo before digging in."

"Yes, that would be wise," Bria said as she walked her patient out into the waiting area and bid her good-bye.

Bria ran her hands through her bouncy, back length curls and headed to her sister's office down the hall. Dr. Raven Arrington, an OBGYN, had just seen her last patient for the day and the two sisters were headed out for their baby sister's bachelorette party.

Bria stuck her head in Raven's partially opened door. "You ready?"

"Yep, let me finish editing this article on advances in infertility treatments," Raven answered, her eyes not wavering from the computer screen and her fingers still moving fast along the keys.

Bria was impressed on how her older sister was always focused, serious-minded and knowledgeable about the medical field and world topics. Bria was more interested in sports, music, good food and fun. She figured once she was out of her twenties---which she had one more year---then maybe she would be more focused and serious-minded like thirty-six year-old Raven. For now, Bria just wanted to enjoy life.

"Did you include something about acupuncture and herbs?"

"Yep." Raven glanced at Bria and then quickly back to the screen. "You know, for someone who is an allergist, you certainly have an interest in naturopathic medicine. Too bad you can't practice it here like you want to, but you know Daddy." Raven ended on a sigh and pushed her naturally curly red hair behind her ear. Her huge gold hoops dangled in the process.

"I can always move to another practice." *Oops.* Bria bit her bottom lip and then pretended to look through her cell phone. She hadn't meant to speak her thought of the past few months out loud, especially to anyone in her family.

"Um...did you forget you are a part owner of our family's practice? Arrington Family Specialists needs you." Raven shut her laptop and placed it in a black leather carrier before she gave her sister a firm gaze.

"I know but...like you said, I have the interest, plus I'm a licensed herbalist, a certified iridologist and a few other things

I haven't shared that I've been working on." Bria shrugged hoping this would be the end of the conversation. She had some possible leads on a job in Atlanta but wasn't ready to discuss it.

"I'm sure you are much to Daddy's dismay."

Their father, Dr. Francis Arrington, a renowned African-American cardiologist and surgeon, had started the practice when Bria was a teenager. Her father wanted his children to work at the family practice, but her heart wasn't strictly in traditional medicine anymore. Instead, she wanted to combine traditional and naturopathic medicine to help her patients with their allergies.

"Raven, let's not discuss this now." Bria's cell phone chimed.

"Let me guess. It's your man." Raven grabbed her coat and proceeded toward the door.

Bria shook her head and glanced at the text. It was her best friend.

"I don't have a man."

"Whatever. Your face lights up whenever your so-called best friend calls or texts you."

"For the last time we're just friends. Besides, he's arrogant, cocky, a jokester, a---"

"A player," Raven interjected, "But you still want him."

Bria sighed. She was tired of her family and close friends insinuating that she liked Rasheed Vincent for more than just a friend. The idea was completely absurd. Because of his player ways and women always after him, she didn't want to fall into the category of being just another notch on his bedpost. No thank you. Instead, they'd become fast friends a few months ago, hanging out at blues clubs and sporting events. She listened to his complaints and trysts about whatever groupie of the week he was seeing. Nope. She liked him, but not enough to put herself in a hurtful situation again.

The sisters bid farewell to the receptionist and walked briskly toward the parking lot in the frigid evening air.

As she sat in the passenger seat of Raven's Mercedes, Bria realized that she never read the text message. His initials, R.V, were in a box on her cell phone. She touched it to see what crazy, off-the-wall thing he had said. The last time she spoke to Rasheed, he was on a private jet going to Las Vegas for the bachelor party for his best friend who was also Bria's sister Shelbi's fiancé. At the time, Bria had to cut the conversation short because of an emergency with a patient. As she read the message, she knew that anything more than a friendship wouldn't work between them.

Wish you were here. A party isn't the same without my home girl by my side. Who else is going to keep my crazy butt in check? Wish me luck. This fine sista with a big butt is checking your boy out.

*****

Rasheed Vincent adjusted his sage-colored bow tie in the mirror as he wondered who had the audacity to pick such a color. He flashed his usual charming, sexy smile that always melted the heart of any woman in the vicinity that had the pleasure of seeing it. A retired, professional basketball player, he enjoyed the attention and company of beautiful women--- until they became too close---and then he was on to the next one.

Rasheed checked his appearance in the mirror one more time. Everything had to be on point today, which wasn't hard for him. His self-confident and slightly arrogant attitude wouldn't let him be anything but on point. His bald head glistened under the vanity lights in the dressing room of the wedding chapel. The Armani tuxedo fit his muscular, athletic physique, showcasing broad shoulders with a rock hard chest and washboard abs. He checked his onyx cuff links and buttoned his tuxedo jacket, before giving himself the thumbs up.

He glanced over his shoulder at his best friend and the groom, Justin Richardson, who was busy reading his wedding vows. Their other best friend and the second best man, Derek

Martin, finished putting on his bow tie and proceeded to open a bottle of Moet.

Rasheed strode over to his boy who in two more hours would no longer be living the single life, something Rasheed never planned to give up. He was a certified playboy and intended to keep it that way.

"You ready to put on that ball and chain...I mean get married and have sex with the same woman for the rest of your life?"

Justin chuckled and placed the paper with the wedding vows in the pocket of his black tuxedo pants. "Of course, I'm ready. I was ready when I first laid eyes on her adorable face."

Derek chimed in, as he poured three glasses of champagne. "Yeah, man I remember. You've been whipped since you met Shelbi."

"I'm not..." Justin paused. "You're right. I am. But my Shelbi is perfect."

Justin and his fiancée, Shelbi Arrington, met just four months before on a trolley in downtown Memphis. Unbeknownst to Shelbi, Justin was the owner and executive chef of the restaurant she had critiqued a few days before for her job as a food critic with the *Memphis Tribune*. After a whirlwind romance, during which Shelbi decided to begin her residency, the couple chose to get married on Christmas Eve. This would give them plenty of time for a honeymoon and a chance move into their new home before Shelbi began her residency in January.

Rasheed checked his Rolex. "Well, if you change your mind, the Bentley is parked out back. I can have the jet ready, and we can be back at the strip club in Vegas in a few hours. Your bachelor party, thanks to me, was off the chain!"

Justin laughed and took the glass of champagne from Derek. "That it was. But now, I'm ready to get married to the most beautiful woman in the world. You know Rasheed, you could be next."

Rasheed almost spit out his champagne and thank goodness he didn't because he knew Shelbi would've had a cow if any stains had been on his tuxedo jacket.

"Married? Naw. Marriage complicates things."

"Really? Like what?" Derek asked.

"Like getting the numbers of all Shelbi's single, hot bridesmaids at the reception." Rasheed took out his cell phone to make sure it was charged. "She even has some fine, sexy twin cousins from Atlanta. Twins! That would be a fantasy come true...again." A wide smile formed on his face.

"How will Bria feel about that?" Justin inquired.

"Bria?" Rasheed wasn't surprised at the question. He had met her at Justin's dinner and blues club a few months ago, and they'd been hanging out ever since. Everyone thought surely they would end up dating, but they were just friends. "Why would she care? She's my home girl. Nothing going on."

Justin and Derek rolled their eyes at each other. A knock sounded on the door, and the men jerked their heads in that direction. Thankful for the interruption, Rasheed motioned to open the door. There stood the topic of their conversation.

"What's up fellas? I have your boutonnières," Bria said as she and Raven entered the dressing room. Raven took a boutonnière from a box in Bria's hand and headed toward Justin.

Rasheed's eyes were instantly drawn to Bria's sexy body like a magnet. The sage-colored, straight dress hugged the curves of her petite five-foot-four frame in all of the right places. His eyes gazed over her hips and a butt that he'd never realized was so rounded. Her small yet plump breasts were sitting up all nice and perky, and he resisted the urge to pull down her dress and introduce himself to them by kneading and kissing them senseless. Her thick, long hair was pinned up in a loose, tousled up do with sexy, wispy curls framing her delicate, bronze face. She always reminded him of the actress Gabrielle Union because of her sexy girl-next-door look.

Rasheed downed his glass of champagne, hoping it would calm down whatever the hell he was feeling for his friend. He tried to concentrate on what Raven blabbed about. Something to do with pictures, rings and walking back down the aisle after the ceremony. But all he could do was imagine hiking up her dress and holding her against the wall. His attention came back when Bria spoke directly to him.

"You're next, playboy," she said in her usual upbeat, bubbly voice.

"Playboy? You think I'm a playboy?" He didn't know why all of sudden he was offended by her comment. She called him that all the time, and he always gave her some witty, smart-aleck answer such as 'and you know this' or 'til the day I die'.

The men and Raven laughed while Bria smiled and shook her head.

"Boy, please." She walked toward him with the rose bud. "The whole world knows you're a playboy. Now, let me put the final finish to your attire so you can take pictures. The photographer is done with Shelbi and the bridesmaids."

"You know," Raven began, "I'm going to go ahead and take Justin down to the chapel now that Shelbi is back in her dressing area. The pastor mentioned wanting to see him."

"Cool. I wanted to ask him a question about the vows I've written," Justin said as he headed toward the door with Raven.

"I'll go with you," Derek said. "I want to get a glimpse of those twins again."

Rasheed looked passed Bria and straight to Derek. "Hey, I got first dibs on the twins," he yelled as the door closed.

"Humph. And you say you aren't a playboy," Bria said with a whispered laugh.

Rasheed looked down at her as she struggled to pin the boutonniere to his lapel. She was on her tippy toes despite the fact that her heels had given her a few extra inches of height. A sweet, soft scent of jasmine and gardenia radiated from her and filled his senses with her aura.

"You smell and look lovely," he whispered in a deep voice that he normally wouldn't use with her. "I'm not used to seeing you all glammed-up. Not that it matters. You would look hot in a potato sack."

Almond-shaped, coffee-colored eyes glanced up at his face, and her lips parted slightly before she sighed and continued to straighten the flower.

"This thing won't stay still!" she expressed in a flustered tone. She unpinned it and tried again.

Rasheed wasn't sure what had ruffled her feathers. Bria was always easy-going and nothing got on her nerves---except the task of pinning the flower to his lapel. When he had first met her, he'd flirted hard. *Real hard.* However, she nipped that in the bud fast. She'd threatened to throw him over the banister of Justin's restaurant and then proceeded to tell him she wasn't some floozy or groupie. After that, he had nothing but respect for her, and they'd hung out ever since going to blues clubs and sporting events as well as playing basketball and bowling. Bria had become one of the boys to him thanks to her athletic ability and easy-going attitude. He still checked her out from time to time, especially in the little shorts she wore when playing basketball or in the sheath dresses she sometimes wore to work. But he never flirted and even asked for advice about whatever chick-of-the-week he was seeing.

"Having problems, Bree?" he asked, using the nickname he gave her and concentrating to stay composed. He tried to remember this was his friend, his home girl. She stood in front of him so close he could see the pulse on the side of her neck beat faster than usual. He pushed his hands in the pockets of his trousers which was pure torture. He really wanted to glide them down her neck, her arms, back, hips, —especially the hips—and then end up on her little plump derriere as he imagined picking her up and kissing her already parted, sexy lips.

"I...I almost got it," she said with a relieved smile. She stuck the pin through the lapel and back out to firmly connect the boutonnière. "Ouch!" She pulled her finger back and waved it in the air.

Rasheed took her finger in his hand and lightly kissed it. Before he had time to think about what he was doing, he sucked the pricked finger into his mouth as his eyes met hers in an intense stare. The rise in his silk boxers strained against his pants as his lips touched her skin. He knew he needed to stop this charade, but her finger was literally finger-licking good, and he wanted more---much more.

"Better?" he whispered in a seductive tone as he caressed her other fingers with his lips.

"Hmm...um..." she stuttered, and her eyes shut as more untamed purrs trailed from her throat.

The aroused music which escaped her was answer enough for him. With little effort, he moved her hands around his neck and drew her small body hard against his. Rasheed bent his head to her quivering lips to imprison them with his. He kissed her slow and deep, relishing in her essence as his tongue wound its way around hers in a slow, sensual dance. Her body arched against his in from what he could tell was pure enjoyment and more soft moans escaped her. He dipped his tongue inside her mouth even further as she continued to reach for it with her own. Her soft hands slid over his bald head, down to his neck and gripped his shoulders which stirred fervor in him.

"You taste so damn good, Bree."

Rasheed had known all along if he ever had the chance to kiss her, she would be delectable. Now he knew what the closest thing to heaven was, and a moan trembled from him. He moved his lips to her smooth neck which released a rumble from her throat. He kissed her with a tenderness that surprised him because he was never one for foreplay, but Bria was a delicate piece of art, and he wanted to treat her as such. He nibbled the hollow area near her collar bone and ran his hands down her backside until they rested on her plump little butt. He was trying his best to not unzip his pants and lift her...

Bria jerked away from him with a gasp and a wide, bewildered gaze. She placed her hand over her mouth as if it were burning.

They stared at each other for a moment before Bria broke the silence. "We need to go," she said in a stern voice he wasn't used to hearing. Usually it was a sweet musical sound, but now it was laced with disapproval and regret.

Coming down from cloud nine, he straightened his tux and looked down at her. Her eyes were wild, lipstick smeared on her full lips, and her breasts rose up and down tempting him to grab her again. He continued to be mesmerized by her hard breathing because one, he caused it and two, her breasts had never looked so perky before. He cocked his head to the side as he realized her nipples poked through the material as if they wanted to break free. How could he have forgotten to touch, kiss, lick, pull and nibble on her two luscious peaches? *Damn. I'm slipping.*

"Bria, are you alright?" He reached for her to offer comfort.

She turned from him and headed towards the vanity area. He placed his hands back in his pockets where they should have stayed in the first place. That's when he realized the monster in his boxers was hard as a rock. He pulled down his tux jacket, but that still didn't hide it.

"I'm fine, but that can't happen again." She blotted the red lipstick with a Kleenex. "We're just friends and friends don't get all hot and bothered for each other."

"So, you're all hot and bothered over me?" He teased trying to make her smile, but the sternness on her face hadn't cracked.

"Rasheed!"

"You're right, Bree. I don't know what came over me." And the truth was he honestly didn't know what had come over him. He couldn't believe the aggressive way he had acted with her.

She headed toward the door avoiding eye contact with him. "Let's just forget this happened. The photographer is ready for the men in the wedding party. You're going to be late, and I don't want Shelbi upset. It's her day today." She opened the door and closed it, leaving him in the room alone.

As much as he loved a passionate kiss with a sexy woman, Rasheed never thought kissing Bria would set his mind into overdrive. Sure, he'd been attracted to her since they'd met. He'd been drawn to her kissable dimples which displayed when she flashed her inviting smile, and he'd had the urge to place kisses in their deep crevices. He loved her funny little laugh, her thoughtfulness and her nonchalant attitude. She was an all around cool woman. She was his best friend, his girl--- he could depend on her to keep him in check and focused. The last thing he wanted to do was upset her. She was visibly shaken when she left, but of course his kisses always did that to any woman. No surprise there.

Rasheed checked himself in the mirror one more time, wiped Bria's lipstick from his lips with his handkerchief and stuffed it neatly back into his pocket. As he opened the door, he realized he was shaken as well, but he wasn't going to let it show. After all he was Rasheed Vincent, player extraordinaire on and off the court. Sure, Bria was beautiful, intelligent and sexy, but he wasn't going to let a woman steal his heart again.

\# 10.99

Made in United States
North Haven, CT
15 April 2022

18301630R00114